The Wedding Date

The Wedding Date

KELLY EADON

FOREVER
YOURS

New York Boston

Forever Yours
Hachette Book Group
1290 Avenue of the Americas
New York, NY 10104
forever-romance.com
twitter.com/foreverromance

First published as an ebook and as a print on demand: April 2016

Forever Yours is an imprint of Grand Central Publishing.
The Forever Yours name and logo are trademarks of Hachette Book Group, Inc.

The publisher is not responsible for websites (or their content) that are not owned by the publisher.

The Hachette Speakers Bureau provides a wide range of authors for speaking events. To find out more, go to www.hachettespeakersbureau.com or call (866) 376-6591.

ISBNs:
978-1-4555-9395-8 (ebook)
978-1-4555-9397-2 (print on demand)

E3

CHAPTER ONE

Music blasted through the elevator. Its low, thumping bass line and bouncing beat made Kate Massie itch to dance.

"Yeah, girl, shake that booty." She could barely make out the muffled lyrics.

Kate couldn't help but grin as she glanced around the elevator. Three men stared back at her, their suits and ties as somber as their expressions. *Whose ring tone is it?* It wasn't the type of thing she expected to hear blaring from the briefcase of a fiftysomething lawyer.

"She's a slut and she knows it. Just like that, uh, uh." The song transitioned to sexual grunting. Kate would have giggled, but all three men continued to stare at her.

That's when she realized.

Holy shit. It must be her phone.

Ryan, one of her best friends, must have changed her ring tone again. That was it, she officially needed to kill him.

Kate glanced at her cavernous bag, which was stuffed to the

brim with her laptop, sunglasses, makeup, granola bars, business cards, and God knew what else, and began to dig through, frantically searching for her kelly green phone case. All of a sudden she felt like Mary freaking Poppins. The X-rated version.

Her cheeks flamed. The song had played for so long it had to be over. *Please let it be over.* By the time Kate found the phone the call had rolled to voice mail.

Stay calm. Kate straightened her shoulders and met each man's gaze, one at a time. All three continued to stare back coldly. She choked back the laughter that bubbled frantically inside her.

"So uh, do you gentlemen have any big plans this weekend?"

One of them grunted something unintelligible and a bead of sweat formed on the back of her neck.

As the elevator came to a halt on the ground floor, the song began to play again. Her stomach dropped.

You've got to be kidding me.

She'd just started this job. She'd see these men every day for the next year, and she refused to let them think she was...well, she wasn't sure what. She had to prove she was poised and in control. *That's what the Notorious RBG would do, right?*

Kate gave a little shimmy and danced her way out of the elevator and into the hall, keeping time with the beat. Then she booked it to her parking space. She never turned to see their faces.

In the safety of her beat-up Toyota sedan, Kate finally allowed herself to dissolve into laughter. When she regained control of herself, she checked her phone. Two missed calls.

One from her sister, Rachel, and the second from Ryan. She wouldn't give him the satisfaction of a response yet.

Kate put on her Bluetooth headset, autodialed her sister, and pulled out of the parking garage.

Rachel answered on the first ring. "Hey! What're you doing?"

"I'm on my way to the gym. You'll never guess what happened." Kate filled her in on the most recent humiliation.

Rachel snorted.

"I know. Ryan got me this time." She'd already begun to plan her revenge. Something involving his beloved Ford Mustang and Silly String. Or maybe penis-shaped glitter. She still had some left from a bachelorette party.

"At least the lawyers know who you are." Her sister's voice was bright.

She flipped on her turn signal and merged onto the highway. Belmont, the beach town where she'd grown up, was only a fifteen-minute drive from the city.

"That's one way of looking at it. I may not have made a good impression, but at least I made an impression."

Rachel laughed again. "Other than your choice of elevator music, how's work?"

She bit her lip. "Mmm, OK, I guess. Kinda boring."

Thanks to the anemic legal job market, Kate had accepted a one-year clerkship for a federal judge. It was prestigious but not what she'd pictured herself doing after law school.

"The economy will pick up, and you'll get a job prosecuting. I know it."

Kate couldn't help but grin at her sister's optimism.

"What are you doing tonight?" Rachel asked.

She found a spot in the line of cars headed for Belmont and flipped on her cruise control. "Not sure yet. Gym, then something."

Her sister sighed loudly. "Kate. It's the weekend. Have fun. I need to live vicariously through you 'cuz I'm an old married fuddy-duddy."

"You'll never be a fuddy-duddy."

Her sister chuckled.

"I'll find something fun to do, I promise."

Rachel's voice turned soft with concern. "I just don't want you to be lonely."

"I know." She'd agonized over her decision to move back to Belmont. Yes, the beach was gorgeous and she had her best friends Ryan and Beth to keep her company, but this wasn't where she'd pictured herself. She'd always dreamed of a glamorous career prosecuting in a big city like New York or Philadelphia.

"What about guys? Have you met any guys?"

Her breath hitched. "There's a ridiculously sexy guy at the gym. Right now I'm content to ogle him."

In fact he'd seduced her in a dream the night before. Imaginary relationships were so much easier than real ones.

There was a long pause. "I want you to be happy again."

Her heart twisted. "I know. And I am happy, Rach. At least I'm as happy as I can be under the circumstances. I'm trying really hard. I promise."

Of all people, her sister understood why she couldn't put down roots here.

"I know you are. I'm proud of you and…"

On her sister's end of the line there was shrieking in the background.

"Ummm, the kids are destroying something. Shit, I gotta go."

"Love you!"

"Love you more!"

Her chest ached as her sister's end of the line went silent. Ever since college she'd had big plans for herself: go to law school, prosecute, and live in a big city near her sister. The plans hadn't worked out. Yet. She resolved to go to the gym and kick, punch, and sweat her way to a better mood, then grab some ice cream for dinner. The two would balance each other out.

When she reached the gym, she parked her car, slung her bag over her shoulder, and jogged to the front door. Only five minutes until kickboxing class, which didn't leave her much time to change. She began to dig through her Mary Poppins bag as she used her hip to push the gym door open. She was still searching for her membership card when she slammed into something solid. A large hand reached out to grip her elbow and kept her balanced.

Someone solid. And delicious smelling. Kate caught the scent of sandalwood, apple, and woods. She tore her attention from the contents of her bag.

"I'm so sorry." She met the man's vivid light-gray eyes.

Her stomach did a flip and the intensity of his gaze sucked the breath from her lungs.

She'd run straight into the headlining star of last night's dream.

* * *

"Are you OK?" James couldn't believe his luck. He'd given up hope of seeing her today and had been leaving the gym when bam, there she was.

His pulse pounded. Of course he'd known her the moment he first saw her. Kate Massie. His date from junior prom. He'd have recognized her long legs and sparkling brown eyes anywhere.

"I'm sorry. I wasn't paying attention." A flush of pink spread across her cheeks. Her forehead furrowed as she stared at him, but she didn't remove her elbow from his grasp. The feel of her soft skin under his fingertips sent a surge of heat through him.

A woman's singsong voice called his name, jerking him back to the present. His jaw tensed and he stepped out of the doorway, pulling Kate with him. Ainsley would recognize her immediately and their brief moment alone would end before it had even started.

Ainsley was out of breath as she rushed up to him. "Thank goodness you haven't left yet. I just remembered I left my lipstick in your car."

She froze, her jaw dropping open as her attention shifted to Kate.

"Ohmygawd!" she squealed. "Katie?"

Kate's eyes narrowed, as if she was trying to place her. So she didn't recognize Ainsley, either.

Then Ainsley enveloped her in a hug. "I can't believe it's you! What are you doing here? Did you finish law school? Did you move back? Where are you working? Where are you living?" The rapid-fire speed of her questions seemed to trigger Kate's memory and she broke into a grin.

God, I love her smile. She was one of those people who smiled with her eyes, not just her lips. Although her lips were equally appealing. He caught himself staring at her mouth and forced his eyes away.

"Ainsley! It's great to see you. Things are pretty good. I finished law school, I moved back, and I'm working for a judge." Her attention flicked back to him and her pupils dilated slightly.

And suddenly his night just got a lot more interesting.

Ainsley placed a hand on his shoulder. "You remember my friend James, right? James Abell, you went to our junior prom with him?"

A smile spread across her face, stoking the fire inside him. Kate hadn't gone to their high school, but she had played soccer with Ainsley. When he'd needed a date at the last minute, Ainsley had recruited her.

"Hey." She reached out to grasp his hand.

Her fingers fit perfectly in his and he waited a long moment before he released them.

"Hey, Kate, it's good to see you again." He'd recognized her the other day and had been working on a plan to reintroduce himself ever since. *Problem solved.*

"Are you going to kickboxing class?" Ainsley motioned down the hall toward the group fitness room.

Kate untangled her gaze from his. "Yeah, it's my first time. I need to change first."

"Yay!" Ainsley clapped her hands. "I'm going, too. We can go together."

This was his chance. He had to act fast.

"We're getting drinks with some friends after this. You should come, Kate."

He and Ainsley met a group of fellow Fallston Prep School graduates for happy hour every Friday night.

Ainsley tugged Kate in the direction of the women's locker room. "Oh, you should come! I'll give you the details."

She shot him another smile. "I'd love to. See you later."

Adrenaline coursed through him. He'd see her later.

CHAPTER TWO

She smoothed back a few sweaty strands of hair and glanced at her reflection in the rearview mirror. At least she'd run into him before her workout and not after.

No way is that James Abell. Absolutely no way.

Her junior prom date had been tall, gangly, and awkward, with bushy hair. Ainsley had practically begged Kate to go with him because he was too shy to ask anyone. He wasn't the least bit awkward anymore. Her face heated all over again as she recalled his tall, well-sculpted body and the way his faded T-shirt outlined his chest muscles.

I bet he has no problem getting dates anymore.

The mere memory of his body launched a primal flutter in her stomach. How ironic that this man, the man from her dream, was the same bumbling boy who'd been too scared to dance with her ten years before.

She took a steadying breath and let herself through the front door of her apartment. Wally threw himself at her, covering her workout clothes with a fine layer of black dog fur. He woofed and wiggled in circles around her legs as she struggled in the direction of her bedroom.

Her childhood best friend and roommate, Beth, sat cross-legged on the living room floor, with fabric and googly eyes strewn around her.

"What are you doing, bunny?" Kate flopped onto the floor next to Beth. She dislodged a piece of felt that had attached itself to her running shoe and handed it back to her friend.

Creative chaos, Beth called it. She was always working on a new project, each one weirder than the last. Her creations littered parts of their dining room table and the living room floor.

Beth dabbed hot glue onto the felt. "Making rat costumes for *The Pied Piper*."

As one of her many part-time jobs, Beth managed Belmont's children's theater.

Kate snickered. "You couldn't find a way to recycle the costumes for *The Three Little Pigs*?"

Last year Kate had spent her spring break constructing pig heads from papier mâché and she still couldn't look at anything pink without having flashbacks.

Beth wrinkled her nose. "Very funny. Do you want to help? I have an extra glue gun around here somewhere."

The invitation gave her the warm fuzzies. The highlight of moving back to Belmont had been the chance to live with Beth.

She fiddled with a piece of felt. "I, um, kind of made plans."

"Oh yeah?" Beth's eyes brightened as she lowered the glue gun. "Do these plans involve a cute guy?"

Kate shot her a look. Why did everyone keep asking that question? Beth, Rachel. They knew she was in Belmont only temporarily. They knew she needed to focus on finding a job as a prosecutor. And they knew how she felt about relationships.

"Well, what does he look like?" Beth was, as usual, impervious to Kate's snarky attitude.

Tall. Handsome. Magnetically sexy and charismatic.

Beth's face lit up as she grabbed Kate's hands. "Is this a date tonight?"

She rolled her eyes. "Of course not. It's like a group thing. Ainsley and her boyfriend will be there, too."

Beth's eyebrows rose at the mention of Ainsley's name, but she said nothing. For the most part they'd hung out with their own public school crowd in high school.

"Does that mean you want me to make you a rat costume to wear?" Beth held up a square of brown felt.

Kate grimaced at the mental image of walking into one of the preppiest bars in town wearing head-to-toe felt and googly eyes.

Beth giggled. "I'm going to take that as a no. Which is a good thing, because I do have a date later and I don't know if I have time to turn you into a rat."

"A date, huh? Who's the lucky guy?" It was her turn to raise an eyebrow.

Beth shrugged. "A guy I met the other week at an art show. He seemed nice."

Oh, Beth. She honestly believed the universe would drop the perfect guy in her lap and it would all work out. Plus she was too nice to turn down dates.

Kate stood from her spot on the floor. She needed to take a shower before going out in public.

"Don't get kidnapped," she called over her shoulder. She closed the bathroom door behind her and turned the shower on full blast.

Tonight was the perfect chance to get out and be social, just as she'd promised Rachel. While she was at it, she might as well harvest some more mental images of James for her late-night fantasies.

* * *

James sidled up to the wooden bar, took the spot next to Ainsley, caught the bartender's eye, and pointed to a local beer on tap.

"Scott's meeting us on his way from work. Who else is coming?" she asked.

"Just us." A lot of their regular group had bowed out for one reason or another: work, family obligations, that kind of thing. Not that he was sorry it would be only the four of them.

"Can you believe Kate Massie is back in Belmont?" Ainsley should have been a social anthropologist. She was obsessed with interpreting social situations and homing in on unspoken social cues.

He took a swig of the beer the bartender plopped in front of him. "Why? She's from here, isn't she?"

He knew Ainsley. If she got any inkling of the way Kate made his blood pound she'd spiral into matchmaker mode. She meant well, but he wasn't in the mood for her meddling.

His mom did enough meddling on the subject of his love life.

Ainsley fiddled with the paper napkin beneath her drink. "I guess. I tried to catch up with her in college, but she said she never came back here anymore."

He was careful to keep his expression neutral. He'd lost track of Kate after junior prom. He should've asked her for her number, but he'd been too shy and tongue-tied in her presence.

That was a long time ago.

It was better not to dwell on what could have happened in the past. He'd turned over a new leaf when he broke up with Brooke and he'd spent the last six months making up for lost time. Literally running into Kate at the gym must have been a sign.

He took another swig of beer and tapped his thumb impatiently against the wooden bar. What time had Ainsley told Kate to arrive? He was ready for her to meet the new James Abell.

CHAPTER THREE

She was reaching for the handle of O'Riley's front door when her phone chimed. She stepped back onto the sidewalk and checked the caller ID. Ryan. Of course. She heaved a sigh. He wouldn't leave her alone until she'd acknowledged his stupid joke.

"You're very funny. My phone went off in an elevator full of lawyers, and I'm already plotting my revenge."

She could practically hear him fist pumping on the other end.

"How many partners? Pretend that you're an announcer at a football game and I'm watching NFL RedZone. Give me every detail, so I can picture it."

Her jaw clenched. She wasn't about to give him the satisfaction of a blow-by-blow. "Three. I'm about to meet some people in a bar. I'll talk to you later?"

"Which bar?" Sure enough, that had distracted him.

"O'Riley's."

"K. I have a date but I might meet up with you." Ryan hung up before she could deter him.

She groaned and leaned against the brick wall. She loved Ryan, but he had a knack for embarrassing her in public. With any luck his date would go well and he'd completely forget about O'Riley's.

Kate walked through the door and spotted Ainsley immediately. Her golden-blond hair fell in gentle waves. She wore a short aquamarine silk dress with gold strappy sandals, delicate gold jewelry, and nail polish that matched her dress.

How did she manage to look perfect when it was 104 degrees?

James and another man stood behind her. Kate's gaze was immediately drawn to James. The sinewy muscles in his forearms made her heart pound. His dark hair curled over the edge of his shirt collar, and his mouth quirked upward in a good-natured smile.

Kate's knees wobbled for a second, but she took a deep breath and walked toward them. *He's just a hot guy.*

Ainsley embraced her. "I'm glad you came! This is so exciting!"

Kate hugged James next. She fit perfectly right below his chin, against his broad chest. He smelled manly, spicy, and she fought the urge to stay buried against his body, inhaling his scent. What was happening to her?

"This is my boyfriend, Scott." Ainsley indicated a blond man with his hair slicked back. Kate tried not to stare at his diamond-studded watch, which had to be worth more than her car. Hell, it was probably worth more than everything she owned combined.

What am I doing here? Her lungs constricted and she had to remind herself to take a deep breath. *Relax and have a good time.*

"There's a spot over here." Ainsley led them to a table in the corner. She'd always reminded Kate of a cruise ship activities director. She planned every social gathering in minute detail and brought unbridled enthusiasm to the most mundane activities.

James pulled out a chair and looked at her, one eyebrow raised. She hesitated. For her? When was the last time a man had pulled out a chair for her? Butterflies filled her stomach and she reached to smooth her hair.

He bent so his mouth was close to her ear and his breath was warm on her neck. "What can I get you to drink?"

Her mind blanked. He wanted to buy her a drink? She never let guys buy her drinks on a first date. But this wasn't a first date.

What could it hurt? She'd let him get this round and she'd get the next.

She swallowed. "I would love a gin and tonic. Thank you."

"Do you have a gin preference?" His mouth was still next to her ear, his deep voice doing funny things to her stomach.

"No, I trust you."

He straightened and grinned. "Famous last words." Then he turned and made his way toward the bar with Scott.

She followed him with her eyes, admiring the wide set of his shoulders and the way his strong legs covered the distance in long strides. When she snapped her attention back to Ainsley the other woman stared at her with a smirk.

Crap. She'd been caught.

Think fast. "Ainsley, how did you meet Scott?"

Ainsley's eyes lit up. "Well, Scott went to Fallston, but he was a few years ahead of me. He was planning an event at the Marjorie Hotel and I was his event planner...."

And she was off. Mission accomplished.

The men returned a few minutes later and James slid Kate's drink in front of her. As he folded his frame into the seat beside her, his leg brushed against hers. Electricity shot through her. Had the contact been intentional? She kept her attention focused on Ainsley, just to be safe.

James rested his arm on the table, inches from hers. "So where are you living? In Belmont?"

She nodded. "My best friend and I found a little bungalow near the public beach. By Pier Twenty-Three."

It had been her favorite pier since her father moved them to Belmont when she was eight. She and Beth had always loved to dangle their feet over the edge and daydream about the small island that was barely visible in the distance.

She watched James's face, waiting for his reaction. Most Fallston-type people lived in the Point. Twenty- and thirtysomethings like James, Ainsley, and Nico lived in the luxury condominium buildings, while people like their parents, and the partners at her law firm, owned mansions along the shoreline. Only townies and tourists lived in the hodgepodge of houses by the public beach.

To her surprise he smiled. No furrowing of the brow and no

downward twist of the lips. Huh. That was it? People at work looked at her as if she had three heads when she told them where she lived.

"Kate," Ainsley interrupted, "have you found a favorite bar yet? Or any good restaurants? A lot of stuff has popped up in the area since you last lived here."

She hesitated. In the few weeks she'd been back she'd spent all her time at work, unpacking boxes, or exploring the beach with Wally. Beth and Ryan tried to keep her busy, but they both had unpredictable work schedules. Wally was the best company, but he was a dog. She couldn't very well take him out for a night on the town.

Ainsley flipped her blond hair over her shoulder. "Don't worry, I'll show you all of the best spots."

Scott tapped her on the hand. "Like Das Beer. We saw that news anchor there last week. The one who lives on that cul-de-sac by your parents."

As they launched into a conversation recounting their celebrity sightings, James angled his body toward her. "How's your sister?"

A flicker of surprise shot through her. "You remember my sister?"

His eyes radiated warmth. "Of course I remember your sister. You used to talk about her a lot. Is she still in Belmont?"

"Nope, Philadelphia. She has two awesome kids now." She pushed aside the dull ache in her ribs and pulled her phone from her purse. "Want to see pictures?"

At that moment a familiar hand pressed against the back of her neck. She froze. Ryan. He'd made it after all. She should subtly pull him aside and tell him to keep his embarrassing Kate stories to a minimum. Things with James were just heating up and she'd strangle him if he ruined it.

"Hey, I've been looking for you." Ryan pulled out a chair and dropped into it. As soon as he sat, James shifted his weight away from her.

So the contact had been intentional. She rubbed her leg, missing his warmth. *Damn you, Ryan.*

"How's your night been so far?" she asked. It was only nine fifteen. It couldn't have gone well.

"Har har, aren't you funny? Introduce me to your friends." He slurred his words slightly.

Great. He was already drunk. Tonight was going to be…interesting.

Under his breath he added, "She didn't look anything like her pictures online."

She stifled a giggle. Beth would say it was karma's way of paying him back for all the practical jokes he'd played on them. And for all the women in Belmont whose phone numbers he'd accidentally "lost."

"This is my friend Ryan. Ryan, this is Ainsley, Scott, and James."

James's eyes hooded and Kate's breath caught. *Oh no, he's not my boyfriend. He's just…Ryan.* Generally speaking, Ryan defied explanation, but they'd been friends for nearly nine years. He was a troublemaker, but he always cheered her up and he planned the best adventures.

Ryan pointedly eyed the empty glass in front of her. "You guys better watch out. Kate's a super-friendly drunk. She'll tell you all the things she likes about you; then she'll tell you her whole life story."

The room had started to take on a lovely haze and she felt as if she were floating on a cloud. That must have been one strong drink.

James smirked. "You want another gin and tonic, Kate?"

She shook her head. "Please, no. I'm good enough at embarrassing myself sober."

He chuckled. "That sounds rather like a promise."

Her cheeks burned. "You wish. This mooch will just drink them all anyway." She jerked a thumb in Ryan's direction.

"Cheers to that." Ryan stood from the table. "Speaking of drinks, I think we all need shots."

As Ryan wobbled his way to the bar, Ainsley reached across the table to grab Kate's hand. "I like him."

Kate quickly waved her away, dismissing the unspoken suggestion. "Oh! No. We're not dating. Ryan is like the super-annoying brother I never had. I could never date him."

Even if there had been chemistry, she didn't date friends. Relationships between friends got serious too quickly, and when they ended, the breakups were always explosive. Her heart twisted at the thought of losing anyone else close to her. No, friendships were precious, which meant they should never be tainted by veering into relationship territory.

Ainsley's face brightened. "Does that mean I can set him up with some of my friends?"

Apparently, as long as they send him realistic pictures before-hand. "Yes, absolutely."

James's leg brushed against hers under the table again. She

let her leg lean against his. After all, what did she have to lose?

Ryan returned with a round of tequila and limes, which he plunked onto the table. He threw back two shots in rapid succession.

He stared at James and his eyes narrowed in concentration. "James. You look really familiar. You into music? Go to shows much?" Ryan owned and operated a small, independent record label.

James frowned. "Not as much as I'd like. Do you row or live in the Meridien in the Point?"

Ryan snapped his fingers. "No…wait, I got it! You know who you look like? That rock-climbing instructor. Kate, you remember him."

She grabbed her shot and threw it back, then wedged the lime into her mouth and bit down.

The date must have been worse than he'd let on. He usually held his liquor well and he was definitely drunk.

Quick! She racked her brain for a witty one-liner or distraction.

Ryan clapped a hand on her shoulder. "You know who I'm talking about. The one you puked all over?"

The muscles in her stomach tensed. As if he'd ever let her forget. She'd made it fifty feet up before she glanced down and lost her lunch all over the instructor. Her aim had been uncanny.

Thanks a lot, Ryan.

Next to her James cleared his throat. "Hey, Ainsley, you're good at wedding stuff. What should I get for my sister for a wedding gift?"

She glanced at him quickly. Was he saving her? He was stone-faced, his expression unreadable. She clenched her hands in her lap.

"Are you thinking something traditional or something more modern? For traditional you could do china and if you want more modern, you could do a nice wine decanter?" Ainsley suggested.

Scott scowled and threw back the rest of his drink. "Just let your girlfriend pick something."

Her gut twisted. James had a girlfriend? How had she misread the signs so badly?

Ainsley shot Scott a pointed look, but he ignored her. *Interesting.* Did Scott have something against weddings in general, or was it a distaste for this wedding in particular?

James clenched the glass in front of him. "Vivian and I aren't dating anymore." That explained the look on Ainsley's face. "My mom had an aneurysm when I told her I was going to attend the wedding without a date." James's mother sounded as overbearing as Kate remembered from their sole encounter.

"You need a date." Ainsley looked to Kate for support. "James's sister is marrying his ex-fiancée's brother in three weeks. It'll be weird if he doesn't bring a date, right?"

Her stomach lurched. Ex-fiancée? Maybe his mother, Margaret, had scared her off. The woman was terrifying.

James grabbed a straw wrapper off the table and crumpled it into a little ball. "We didn't have that kind of breakup. We're friends. We get along."

Under the table she shifted her leg away from his. This sounded complicated.

Ainsley sighed. "Brooke will be there with her new fiancé. No matter how well you get along, if you go stag, it'll attract a lot of attention and gossip. I'm sure I know someone you can take." Her blue eyes darted to Kate.

Ryan poked her in the side, but she ignored him. It was a terrible idea. A family wedding was not a low-key first date. It would only lead to awkwardness, expectations, and pressure.

James's voice was gruff. "I'm not taking a date. I'll be busy as a groomsman and if we survive without my mom and sister killing each other, it'll be a major accomplishment for the family."

Good. They were agreed then.

"You should take Kate," Ryan slurred.

The muscles in her neck tensed.

Was there no limit to the amount of trouble Ryan could cause in one day? When he sobered up, he'd be the first to admit he deserved cruel and unusual punishment.

"I couldn't ask that of her again. She rescued me once in high school and I'm sure once was more than enough for her." James avoided her gaze. He was right, but his lame excuse still stung. She'd been his date only once, almost ten years ago.

Alcohol and pride seized Kate's tongue. "I'm an amazing fake wedding date, and parents love me."

The moment the words were out of her mouth she wanted to snatch them back. Why had she said that? A family wedding would be the worst first date ever. Sure, she wanted to see James again, but…

James's jaw ticced as he reached for her hand. "If you want

to come and it wouldn't be an inconvenience, then I'd love for you to be my wedding date."

Her spine went rigid. She'd backed him into a corner and there was no way to escape now. Why did she always open her mouth without thinking?

"It's not a big deal." She punctuated the words with a self-conscious shrug.

"It's a big deal to me." His thumb grazed the top of her hand, sending goose bumps up her arms.

The rest of their group stared at them.

Kate pulled her hand free and nodded curtly. "Sounds like a plan. You just let me know when and where and I'll be there."

Ainsley squealed in excitement. It was a habit she apparently hadn't outgrown. "Ohmygosh, can I dress you?"

"Sure." Ainsley had excellent taste and Kate had already committed to this disaster. She might as well look good while she avoided his mother and ex-fiancée.

Ainsley turned her focus to James. "I need you to send me the color of the bridesmaid dresses and the venue and time so I can figure out the right outfit. Or maybe send me your mom's e-mail and I can coordinate with her…"

Unease knotted Kate's stomach. "Wait, you're not going?"

Mentally she kicked herself.

"Nope." Ainsley rolled her eyes. "They cut the guest list at one thousand."

Kate's eyes strained, feeling as if they might pop out of her head. *One thousand?* She wouldn't know anyone other than James and his mother.

Crap shit damn. It was too late to back out now. She'd just have to channel her inner RBG and power through.

She signaled the server for another drink. She'd take an Uber home.

* * *

The next morning James stood in the shower and let the scalding-hot water pummel him.

He squeezed his eyes shut and recalled the image of Kate as she'd walked into the bar last night. Her long, silky hair had flowed over her shoulders and her dark eyes had sparkled when she spotted him. Her racerback dress had given him an unobstructed view of her toned shoulders and the smattering of freckles that dotted her skin. The memory was enough to make him hard and he groaned in frustration.

I have to find a way out of this.

He'd pictured her sitting across the table from him at a restaurant, her eyes dancing as she laughed at his jokes. He'd imagined the way her mouth would taste, the way his hands would skim over her body. He'd never envisioned her sitting at a table with his family while his mother harped about her desire for grandchildren and his ex, Brooke, watched them anxiously from across the room.

His temple pounded. This would be a disaster. Dating was supposed to be fun. Dating Kate would be fun. He could get to know her on his own time and enjoy her company, without any pressure. He'd just gotten out of a nine-year relationship, after all, and he didn't want to jump into anything serious.

He sighed and scrubbed his hair vigorously. His mom was

the very definition of pressure. She expected him to bring a date to the wedding and he couldn't hold her off forever. Just as she expected him to have an extravagant wedding at the Belmont country club, buy a house in the Point, and have babies. That was what their family did. His brother and sister were on track with their mom's plan, but he'd jumped the rails when he broke up with Brooke. How long would it take her to realize he wasn't getting back on her crazy train?

He stepped out of the shower and toweled off his hair. The buzzer for his apartment interrupted his thoughts. *Bzz. Bzz. Bzz. Bzz.* Speak of the devil. His mother believed that the more urgently she pushed the buzzer, the faster he'd open the door.

He wrapped a towel around his waist and went to the door. Sure enough, his mother showed up on the video monitor. He pushed the button to grant her access. This was why he hadn't given her a key. She considered it her right to drop by unannounced.

By the time she reached the door of his apartment, he'd thrown on clothes and set the coffeepot to brew.

"Hello, Mother." He kissed her cheek.

"What took you so long? I've been waiting outside forever." She breezed past him and settled herself on the sofa.

"I was in the shower. I didn't know you were coming by."

She huffed dramatically. "I didn't know I was coming by, either. But then I ran into Ainsley, and you didn't answer your phone. As usual. I had no choice."

He collected a few dirty glasses from the coffee table and deposited them in the sink. "Sorry about that. You shouldn't have gone out of your way. Want some coffee?"

She blinked at him incredulously. "Of course I want coffee, but that's not why I'm here. Do you have something you want to tell me?"

He rattled through the cupboards, found a pair of coffee mugs, and poured. It was a rhetorical question. She was here for a specific reason and he'd just have to wait for his tongue-lashing to discover it.

She accepted the mug he held out to her, read the side, then made a face. "You really should get new dishes, honey. Something matching."

He let the comment pass. He'd purposely given her the mug with "Bite Me" emblazoned across the side.

She crossed one leg over the other. "I ran into Ainsley at the store this morning. We were talking about Morgan's wedding and your whole date situation. Anyway, you won't believe what Ainsley told me."

"What?" He knew better than to try to participate in the conversation.

"She told me you're seeing someone."

His hand jerked, sloshing coffee down the front of his shirt. "She said what?"

Anger ripped through him. Had Ainsley lost her mind? It wasn't like her to lie, especially not to his mother. They'd been friends since the first grade and she'd always been afraid of his mother. With good reason.

She tapped a manicured nail on the side of her cup. "Yes. She said you've been dating this girl for weeks, which I know is impossible because you never said anything to me."

Acid churned in his stomach. Was this some kind of joke? He considered his words carefully before he spoke. "Who did Ainsley say I was dating?'

"That girl, what's her name. The one from high school. The one you went to prom with."

His blood ran cold. *Ainsley told her I'm dating Kate?* "Kate?"

"Yes! That's her. Kate."

He gulped down some coffee, burning his throat. Not that he gave a damn. What had Ainsley been thinking? She knew they weren't dating. She knew his mother would dig her talons into this fantasy relationship and refuse to let go.

Ainsley had a reason—she must. He needed to get his mother out of here and call her, so he could figure out what was going on and how to fix it. Immediately. He couldn't ask Kate to pretend to be his girlfriend, too. That was entirely too pathetic.

"Well?" his mother prompted.

He gritted his teeth. "Well what?"

She released a long, measured breath. "Why didn't you say anything? I'm your mother, for goodness' sake. Your mother shouldn't find out about your girlfriend at the grocery store."

"It's complicated." How to explain this to her? He couldn't puzzle it out himself. What exactly had Ainsley said and why?

"Ever since you broke up with Brooke you've been…unfocused. You need to find a woman, get married, buy a house, and have kids. Don't you want those things?"

"I. Don't. Know." He practically spit the words. Why was that so hard to understand? He'd been in a committed relationship since he was eighteen. What was wrong with wanting to date different women?

Everyone in his family had married their high school sweethearts going back generations, but that didn't mean he wanted to join their ranks.

She pursed her lips, as if she'd tasted something sour. "Does Kate know that? Women don't like to have their time wasted."

He clenched the handle of his coffee mug. "Don't worry about it."

He didn't have the energy for this. A Mom interrogation could last for hours.

Her face reddened. "You're not going to tell me anything about her?"

He bit back a smile. Now that was a tempting possibility. "She's a lawyer. She grew up in Belmont. And you'd better be nice to her."

She made a strangled sound in the back of her throat. "Of course I'll be nice to her. Why wouldn't I?"

"Mother." His tone held a thinly veiled warning. She'd never liked anyone he'd dated. Ever since Brooke he'd tried to keep his girlfriends away from her, with varying degrees of success.

She folded her hands tightly in her lap. "I only want what's best for you."

"But I get to decide what's best for me."

He couldn't suppress his smile. Maybe he should challenge her more often. It felt pretty damn good.

A moment later she was back to her normal self. "Since she's your girlfriend, we need to meet her as soon as possible. Invite her to the family dinner on Thursday. And the rehearsal dinner. Of course she'll need to stay at the hotel, with the rest of the family, so she can be there for all the events."

His spine went rigid. He wanted to take her on a date, not scar her for life. That was way too much time with anyone's family, but especially his.

"She's a lawyer, Mom, she has a life and she's busy. There's no way she'll be able to make it to all those events on such short notice."

Her eyes focused on him like laser beams. "If you'd told me earlier, it wouldn't be short notice. Besides, I can get her number from Ainsley and I know Kate wouldn't say no to me. Women want their future mothers-in-law to like them."

The beginnings of a migraine slammed into the base of his neck. This morning he hadn't thought the situation could get worse. Then his mom had arrived.

He dug a thumb into his temple, desperate to relieve the pounding in his head. This was his mother. He'd been naïve to think he could handle her on the subject of wedding dates and keeping up appearances. He would have to call Kate and cancel the whole thing. He couldn't subject her to the loony bin he called a family.

He'd get through the wedding, wait a few weeks, and ask her out on a normal date. And he'd never allow his mother within ten feet of her.

CHAPTER FOUR

Kate sprawled next to Beth in one of the lounge chairs in their backyard as Wally galumphed through the sand. The roar of the nearby ocean soothed her, while the tall privacy fence hid them from prying tourist eyes.

There was nothing like nursing a hangover with her best friend, her dog, and a cool glass of homemade kombucha. She'd wanted to add a shot of vodka, hair of the dog and all that, but Beth would have been offended. It hurt her heart to see her tea recipe adulterated.

Beth lowered her giant retro sunglasses to peer at Kate. "So you're going to a wedding with shy-turned-sexy James? I told you the universe works in mysterious ways."

Kate scrunched her nose in response. "You sound like the back of a romance novel. You can't call him shy-turned-sexy James. He's just regular I'm-going-to-his-sister's-wedding-as-his-date James."

Beth made a sound in the back of her throat. "Regular, huh?

I thought you said he was…hmm, I wanna make sure I get your words right here. 'Kinda sexy.'"

Kate's face heated. Of course Beth had seen right through her attempt at nonchalance. The truth was, she had no idea what to think about the whole thing. It had "big fat mistake" written all over it, but a part of her thrilled at the idea of seeing James again.

Masochist.

Beth touched a finger to her lip and feigned deep thought. "That's exactly what I thought. He's sexy. You're going to his sister's wedding. Someone tell me why I shouldn't be excited for you?"

"It's not a real date. I'm going to party all night with his family while his ex-fiancée sizes me up." Her voice was dry.

She was pretty sure the invitation placed her firmly in the friend zone. Sure there were sparks, but the whole situation was too awkward and strange to develop into something else. She should accept right now that he was just a friend.

Beth sat up in her chair and folded her legs under herself. "What are you thinking? I can see the gears turning."

She drained her glass. "I'm thinking I need more caffeine if we're going to have this conversation right now. Where's Ryan?"

He'd texted almost thirty minutes ago, promising to bring her apology coffee and gluten-free maple bacon doughnuts from Little Ray's coffee shop. To her surprise he'd remembered last night, which meant he understood the necessity for an apology. A good apology.

Beth flapped one hand in the air. "Don't change the subject.

Explain to me why you're not excited about a date with a hot guy."

She sucked in a deep breath. Where to start? "He's not my type."

Beth's lips turned downward. "Since when is really sexy not your type? I don't buy it. Try again."

Fine. "He reminds me of Nico."

Beth cocked her head to the side. "And what about that scares you?"

Kate pulled a face. It was only 9:00 a.m. and she was hungover. Did they really have to do best friend free therapy right now?

Beth grabbed her hand and squeezed. "Seriously. Dig deep. Get it all out there. You'll feel lighter."

Kate took a deep breath. "I feel like I'm a hot mess. And I'm lonely." Her chest ached. Her mom had left before she was four and her dad had died when she was sixteen, after a long battle with cancer. Ever since, she'd been terrified of loneliness. Missing her parents was already physically painful. Being alone made their absence hurt even more.

"I'll give you this—you do have shitty taste in men."

Kate giggled. "Thanks for the vote of confidence."

Beth shrugged. "Nico was too straitlaced. He wanted you to be some cookie-cutter version of the perfect Stepford girlfriend." Her forehead furrowed. "Honestly, bunny, I can't remember the last halfway decent guy you dated."

She groaned out loud and lifted her arms to cover her face. This was already too deep for her. The corners of her eyes pricked. If she wasn't careful she'd cry. And she never cried.

"That's the thing. I don't want to date. Too messy. Too complicated. Besides, what the hell do I need a man for anyway?"

Beth wiggled an eyebrow. "Sex?"

Kate smacked her playfully with one hand. "Need I remind you that one doesn't have to date in order to have sex?"

Beth blushed, which made her giggle. "But you're going to the wedding with James, right?"

She leaned back in the lounge chair and stretched her arms over her head. "I guess. I did convince him to invite me. No idea why I did that, by the way. But it's not a real date." In the sober light of day, she knew she couldn't let herself be interested in James. They were connected in too many little ways. It was bound to get complicated and Belmont was only so big. To date him would be to invite more disaster into her life, right when she was supposed to be getting things back on track.

Beth sighed. "Like I said, that's bullshit. Just promise me you'll go and you'll keep an open mind. You never know what might happen."

The trill of Kate's phone interrupted their conversation. She'd changed it to a normal ring tone and added the fingerprint lock, to keep Ryan out permanently. Ainsley's name flashed across the screen.

An uneasy feeling settled in her stomach, but she answered anyway. "Hey, Ainsley, how are you?"

On the other end, Ainsley was breathless. "I'm good. Look, I ran into James's mom at Piccolo's this morning, and I kind of said something, but I think it's going to be OK." Of course they both shopped at the city's poshest grocery store.

Tiny pinpricks of worry formed inside her. What had Ainsley done? She held her breath and waited for the bombshell to drop.

"She was going on and on about the wedding and how Brooke, James's old fiancée, just got engaged and how she's worried James will never settle down and everyone will feel sorry for him at the wedding because he'll be all alone. She asked if I knew of anyone to set him up with." Ainsley raced through the words a mile a minute.

Kate chewed on her bottom lip. Why did James's mom have to be such a ridiculous busybody?

"You know how Margaret is. She was being bossy, telling me all the reasons James needs a girlfriend and what kind of girl I should find for him. James is the best guy, but she won't cut him any slack. Margaret acts like there's something wrong with him because he isn't married."

"Mmmhmm." When would she get to the point? Kate had seen James, she knew as well as everyone else that he was capable of finding a girlfriend. Was this a convoluted attempt by Ainsley to rescind the invitation from last night?

A knot formed in her stomach. She didn't really want to go, but she'd wanted him to want her to go. *That makes no sense.*

There was a long pause. "Since you said you'd go to the wedding with him, I didn't think it would be *too* much of a stretch, so I told Margaret you're his girlfriend."

She nearly dropped the phone. "Wait—what? Shit!" The words flew out of her mouth before she could think. "Why would you do that, Ainsley?"

Being someone's wedding date was one thing, but pretending to be his girlfriend was entirely different.

Ainsley's voice grew quieter, and more subdued. "I knew you wouldn't mind, and I felt bad for him. It's a messy situation, and he's my friend. Plus she made me so mad, I couldn't help myself."

She dropped her forehead into her hands. If James wanted to let his mom run his life, that was his business. *I, however, have no desire to get sucked into the* Mommie Dearest *tornado.*

Beth eyed her quizzically and she had to remind herself to breathe. *In and out.* There had to be an easy way out of this, where nobody's pride got hurt.

"Did you tell James?" He'd know immediately that this was a bad idea and he'd straighten it out. Ainsley was his friend, which meant he should be the one to clear this up.

"Ummmm." There was a long silence on the other end and Kate's stomach twisted. Ainsley hadn't told him. "Look, you don't know Margaret. His mother is on his case all the time. Normally he just ignores her, but his little sister's wedding and his ex-fiancée's engagement have put his mother on the warpath. This is the only way to get Margaret to back off. Then, after the wedding, you guys can break up or whatever. He and Vivian stopped seeing each other a few weeks ago. I told her that's how long you've been dating."

A few weeks? Kate's mind reeled. "You want me to invent an entire relationship?" she hissed.

"Please." Ainsley's voice was almost a whisper. "He's my friend and he's a really good guy. He'll tell me this whole thing is crazy and I should mind my own business, but I saw you two the other night. If you go with him, it will get his mom off his back and I know you'll have a good time. Just give it a chance. As a favor to me."

Kate clenched her fingers tighter, counted to ten, and let out a deep breath. How had she gotten sucked into this? She couldn't unload all her emotional baggage on Ainsley the way she did with Beth.

She glanced at Beth, who stared at her with wide eyes. Maybe it was better this way. Maybe spending time with his family and his ex-fiancée would shore up the defenses his gray eyes and broad chest had started to erode. Once she got a glimpse of his personal drama, he wouldn't seem so sexy.

"Fine. I'll go to the wedding and pretend to be James's girl-friend."

Am I still drunk?

Ainsley squealed. "When do you want to look at dresses? I'll come by and we can choose a few. We need to figure out how to do your hair, jewelry, and makeup. Oh, and we need to schedule a full manicure and pedicure."

Apprehension welled up inside her. "Who else knows about this? I mean, who else thinks we're dating?"

It suddenly occurred to her that there were people at the courthouse where she worked who had gone to Fallston. Would she be expected to play the part all the time, or just for the weekend? How convincing did her performance need to be?

Just the thought made her heart race. Maybe she'd get to kiss him after all, if only for the sake of authenticity. As long as they both knew they were playing parts, it should be easy enough to keep real emotion out of it. Maybe this would work out to her advantage—no commitment, no strings attached, after all.

There was a long, unnerving pause. "Well, um…if Margaret knows, pretty much everyone knows. I'm sure she made sure it got back to Brooke's mom as soon as possible."

Her throat went dry. Of course. For people like Margaret, image was everything. No wonder Ainsley had called to convince her before she broke the news to James. There really was no way out of this.

The back screen door slammed as Ryan strode into the yard. "I come bearing gluten-free doughnuts and cappuccinos. I'm so sorry, please forgive me, don't make me beg."

He gave her a sheepish look from beneath his shaggy blond hair. It was one of his better apologies. Normally he just muttered, "I'm sorry. Are you happy now?" and shoved a doughnut at her.

She let her head flop back against the lounge chair. He'd started this disaster, which meant he owed her a hell of a lot more than doughnuts. "Ainsley, I have to go. Ryan just got here with my apology doughnuts."

Ainsley gave a bark of laughter. "Apology doughnuts?"

As long as she and Ryan had been friends, they'd had apology doughnuts. It was one of their routines. When she was diagnosed with gluten intolerance, he'd even found a coffee shop that sold gluten-free baked goods.

Sometimes he was thoughtful, for a Neanderthal.

"He owes me doughnuts for telling the puke story last night. And for volunteering me to go…" She trailed off. "It's just a thing we do." On second thought, today's doughnuts should count only for the elevator incident.

"Oh well, I guess I owe you doughnuts now! For this whole girlfriend thing." Ainsley's voice was bright and cheery.

A prickling sensation crawled along her neck.

"That's OK, Ainsley. I have to go, though, I'll see you later." She accepted her cappuccino from Ryan and took a sip. Delicious. Completely worth the phone-in-the-elevator incident, almost worth the wedding date volunteerism, and not at all worth the fake relationship.

"OK, bye! I'll call you later this week so we can work out details." Ainsley clicked off.

She punched the off button and dropped her phone onto a beach towel. Ryan grinned at her. "Well, what did Ainsley say?"

It hit her then, like a train.

She'd been set up. Ainsley was matchmaking and she'd fallen for it, hook, line and sinker.

And now she was officially James Abell's pretend girlfriend.

CHAPTER FIVE

His muscles strained as he heaved the barbell into the air. "Eleven."

One more rep. Sweat poured down his face as he lifted one more time, the relief of exertion and fatigue numbing his brain.

"Twelve."

The moment his mother left he'd called Ainsley. After a halfhearted apology she'd said, "I saw you two making eyes at each other all night. This just expedites the inevitable. Besides, she didn't mind at all. Doesn't that say something?"

Ainsley meant well, she really did, but he couldn't deal with her right now. He needed an hour or two to clear his head and regain control.

His spotter lifted the bar and placed it back in the rack. James sat up on the bench and took a swig from his water bottle.

"Take five?" He needed a short break, then it would be his chance to spot.

A figure across the room caught his attention. Long, lean legs, perky butt, toned shoulders, and dark, sleek hair.

His pulse pounded in his ears as he caught her dark eyes staring.

She lifted a hand in a small wave.

Shit. That was Belmont for you. He'd come to the gym to forget her.

He wouldn't pretend that Kate was his girlfriend. There was an order you were supposed to follow. First you asked a woman out. If that went well, you kissed her and asked her out again. After a few dates you might ask her to be your girlfriend and after a few months you might let your parents meet her. You didn't meet her, immediately call her your girlfriend, drag her to your sister's wedding, and share a table with your ex-fiancée.

When he'd seen her in the gym the other night, this wasn't how he'd imagined everything playing out. He thought he'd ask her to dinner, where they'd chat and laugh. At the end of the night he'd wrap his arms around her slim waist and kiss her on the mouth as her body melted into his. Then they'd play it by ear.

He didn't want or need a girlfriend, no matter what his mother thought. He just wanted to date. He'd been in a committed relationship since he was eighteen. Was a little freedom so much to ask for?

She crossed the room and stood in front of him. "Hey."

He was aware of her gaze on his chest.

"Hey." His throat constricted. "You don't have to do this." It came out as a growl. Not at all what he'd intended. "You don't have to"—he dropped the volume of his voice and stepped closer to her—"pretend to be my girlfriend. You don't have to do that. It's crazy."

Her eyes widened.

Then she lifted a hand and rested it on his shoulder.

"You need a date, right?"

He gave a sharp nod. The truth was, he did kind of need a date for the wedding.

"And your mom thinks I'm your girlfriend, right?"

His breathing was sharp and ragged to his own ears. He nodded again.

"Then we might as well do this." She let her hand drop and gave him a small smile.

Adrenaline pumped through his veins. "I don't want you to be forced into anything. She's my mother, I can handle her."

She gave a sharp laugh. "I know you can handle her, but isn't this what friends are for?" She bit her lip. "I don't have much family, so my friendships are really important to me. To me this is the kind of thing you do for a friend."

Friends. Her words tore through him, leaving him deflated.

He slumped a little and rubbed a hand over the stubble on his chin. This was one hell of a favor. "Then the least you could do is let me buy you dinner. Monday night?"

Her lips parted, but no words came out. Her silence hung heavy in the air, weighing on him.

"As friends," he quickly added. "If you're going to pretend to be my girlfriend, we might as well learn a little more about each other. My mom can be tough to fool."

Her shoulders relaxed and one side of her mouth quirked up. "OK. I like a challenge. I'll be the most convincing fake girlfriend you've ever met. Your mom won't know what hit her."

He forced himself to return her smile, despite the disappointment churning inside him.

What did you expect? Of course she didn't want to go on a real date. That would only complicate things further. Besides, he'd learned over the last nine months that most women wanted a commitment he wasn't prepared to offer. It was probably better this way.

Her eyes swept over his face. "I'll see you Monday?"

"Yeah. I'll see you Monday."

Friends. It was better than nothing.

* * *

Holy shit. Waves of heat rolled over her and she hadn't even set foot on a piece of exercise equipment.

The minute she walked into the gym and saw him, she could have sworn her heart stopped. There he stood, disheveled hair framing his face, his T-shirt tight with sweat across his muscular chest. She'd spent the whole conversation painfully aware of every inch of his body.

It's just the pheromones. She closed her eyes and tried to center.

When her stomach finally stopped jumping, she chose a treadmill facing away from him and hopped on. There was only one way to get this out of her system: a nice long workout.

She popped her headphones on and cranked up the old-school heavy metal. Angry music helped her run faster.

He'd given her an out and she hadn't taken it. Why hadn't she taken it?

If she bailed on him now, he'd be embarrassed in front of his mother and everyone they knew. She couldn't do that to him.

She punched a button on the treadmill, gradually increasing her speed.

And Beth was right. She was lonely. This charade would get her out of the house and give her a chance to meet new people. Plus they both knew it was pretend, which meant they didn't have to deal with unrealistic expectations or misunderstandings. She wouldn't actually get emotionally invested, so there was no risk of being hurt. Meanwhile she'd get to admire James and his rock-hard body.

Win-win.

Besides, she'd spent twenty-eight years dutifully following the path she'd laid out for herself and she'd still hit giant potholes along the way. For once she could take a little detour and do something unexpected.

Something that didn't involve heights.

Her phone chimed through the headphones and a message flashed across the screen.

Ugh. Nico.

Nico: I'm in Belmont for a few days. Want to meet up?

She eyed the message. Should she respond or should she ignore? She didn't believe in staying friends with exes. It was always awkward and weird. She'd been unequivocal when she broke up with him, telling him they didn't want the same things and she couldn't see a future for them together. Why couldn't he accept that? Why was he still texting nearly five months later?

She grabbed the phone and typed quickly.

Kate: I don't think that's a good idea.

It was rude to ignore him. If she was polite but firm he'd get the message eventually. Nico was used to getting what he wanted, whether it was her or a job at his dad's finance firm for when he graduated business school.

Nico: Why not?

She wanted to reach through the phone and throttle him.

Then it hit her. For the next week at least, James was her pretend boyfriend. Subtlety hadn't gotten her anywhere. It was time for a new tactic.

Kate: I'm seeing someone.

Three dots appeared, signaling he was drafting a message. After another moment it chimed through.

Nico: Who?

His word set her blood on fire.

She typed before she could think better of it.

Kate: It's none of your business. Please don't message me any-more.

There. Maybe he'd finally knock it off.

CHAPTER SIX

She gave her hair one more pass with the brush and glanced in the mirror.

This isn't a date. So why did it matter how she looked?

Her heart did a little tap dance. It mattered because James would arrive any minute to pick her up for dinner. The doorbell rang and Wally launched into his happy dance. His back half flopped from side to side, and his giant fluffy tail whipped through the air.

"Sit." She pointed a finger at him and he immediately dropped his rear. That was another benefit to adopting an adult dog. They came fully trained.

She twisted the doorknob and pulled it open.

The sight of him tied her in knots. He was gorgeous in his khakis and a button-down shirt with the sleeves rolled up. A day's worth of stubble dotted his chin and his gray eyes drank her in.

The room spun for a second. Without thinking she stepped

forward to inhale his masculine, sandalwood-tinged scent and gripped his arm for support. She stared at him and fumbled for something to say. She could have sworn his lips were drawing her in, daring her to taste them.

Her stomach lurched and she dropped her eyes to the ground.

Not a date. She took a step back, then spun to grab her purse.

"Is this your dog?" The low rumble of his voice made her pulse skip.

She steeled herself before she turned her attention back to him. "Yes. This is Wally."

People loved Wally. He was big enough to look intimidating but worked himself into a state of pure bliss every time he encountered a person. The only threat with Wally was the possibility of being accidentally whipped by his wagging tail.

"What kind of dog is he?" James knelt and Wally rested his head on James's shoulder.

"Ummm, big fluffy black dog?" People asked all the time, and it was the best answer she'd been able to come up with. "There's a rescue in New Jersey called Last Chance Resort. They pull dogs from high-kill shelters in the South and transport them for adoption. I saw his face on their Facebook page and fell head over heels in love. They helped me adopt him and now he's my baby." She leaned over and rubbed Wally's soft ears. He'd come closer to running out of time than she liked to think about.

"Was his name always Wally?"

Kate patted his thick fur. "Nope. He used to hide a lot,

but he's so big, he'd bury his head somewhere and think we couldn't see the rest of him. I named him after *Where's Waldo?* because he'd always hide with his big fuzzy butt hanging out."

He chuckled. "That's one of the best dog names I've ever heard."

Her face heated and she stared at her purse strap as she wound and unwound it around her hand. "Thanks."

"All right, big man." James scratched Wally's ears. "Your mom and I need to head out."

Kate's heart skipped a beat. Few people understood her bond with Wally. In the last two years he'd become her best friend. Wally understood her and he'd gotten her through a tough period. It wasn't the same as having a child, by any stretch, but Wally was her family. And Kate had very little family.

She followed him onto the porch and locked the door behind her. "Where are we going?"

James flashed a grin. "It's a surprise."

For a second she was lost in his eyes. They were piercing gray, but when he joked and smiled, they appeared lighter.

Then he turned to the car and she came crashing back down to earth. *Get a grip.*

He led her to the Range Rover parked on her street, opened the passenger door, and held out his hand to help her in. The warmth of his skin on hers was enough to make her heart race. How was she supposed to get through the next week without melting into a puddle of desire?

Clearly I need to get laid. She'd walked away from Nico right before graduation, and the sex had never been mind-blowing. Yet another reason she should have ended the relationship sooner.

She took a deep breath and let it out slowly. She could do this. She sneaked a peek at James, whose attention was fixed on the road.

Just friends. She'd made the agreement very explicit.

He pulled the car onto a small side street in downtown Belmont. The blinking neon sign outside announced "Sushi." A restaurant without an actual name. Interesting. This was already shaping up to be an adventure.

While she gathered her purse, James jumped from the car, ran around to the passenger door, and opened it. He held out his hand to help her down and she accepted it. The Land Rover was awfully high up, after all.

She fell into step beside him as they crossed the street to the restaurant.

His phone trilled. James pulled it from his pocket and glanced at the screen.

His mouth twisted. "I'm sorry, I have to take this quickly. Do you mind if I join you inside in a minute?"

She didn't mean to look, but her gaze slipped downward and the letters practically punched her in the face.

Brooke.

Her stomach hollowed out. She jerked her eyes away and headed for the door to the restaurant. "Absolutely. I'll grab us a table."

She tried to quash the anxiety that welled up inside her. She was just a friend. His relationship with his ex was none of her business.

A hostess dressed in jeans and a black T-shirt led her into a small dining room with wooden tables and sat her in the back, so she faced the door. James entered a few minutes later, strode across the room, and dropped into the seat across from her. "Sorry about that. Family stuff."

Her spine prickled. Family stuff? She'd seen Brooke's name on the phone. Why would he lie?

"No problem." She kept her attention on the twenty-page menu, half of which was in Japanese. She tried to focus, but its volume was overwhelming. What on earth should she order?

He flipped his menu open. "I hope you like sushi. I come here all the time. They have the best sushi in the state."

She grinned at him and snapped her menu closed again. "Good. Since you're the expert, why don't you pick some things and I'll try whatever you think is good. I trust you."

James's eyes twinkled. "I don't know. That seems like a lot of pressure. Is there anything you don't eat?"

Crap. She'd forgotten to tell him she didn't eat gluten. She was so used to it, she rarely thought about it anymore. "No gluten stuff."

His mouth thinned. "Ah, my mom swears by the gluten-free diet, too. She's been making Morgan do it to lose weight for the wedding."

Ugh, she hated that. When had her illness become a fad diet? "Oh, I wish it was a dieting thing. I'd gladly weigh more if I could eat bread. It makes me puke. I guess it works for weight loss, but it's not worth it for me."

He rested his elbows on the table and leaned forward, the smile back on his lips. "Is gluten-free food any good? They have cookies and crackers in the store, and it seems like restaurants have gluten-free pizza and all that. I always wonder if they taste like cardboard."

She wrinkled her nose. Honestly, a lot of it did resemble cardboard more than food. "Some of it's great, some of it sucks. Best thing is rice is gluten-free. I *love* sushi."

"I bet I could make you some really good gluten-free bread." He held her eyes and her stomach flipped.

Stop it. Friends could make bread for other friends. Besides, he was clearly still hung up on his ex. Everything about the situation said beware. She knew better than to fall into a relationship that was doomed to failure. At least she liked to think she did.

The waitress appeared next to the table, her notepad in hand. "Are you two ready?"

"Yes." James handed her both menus, stacked together. "We would like the sushi boat for two with whatever the chef recommends."

He beamed at Kate. "I hope you're hungry. It's a lot of food."

"Oh, I can eat a *lot* of food." She abruptly shifted her gaze to the table, picked up her chopsticks, and toyed with them. She was here for a reason and it wasn't to flirt. "Anyway, we should talk about the wedding. It will be a big test on how well I know you and I want to be convincing. You'd better fill me in on all the gory details."

He rubbed the stubble on his chin. "How gory?"

She snapped the chopsticks apart and twirled them in her fingers. "How long have we been dating?

"I think Ainsley told my mother a few weeks." James frowned.

She needed to try harder to keep this lighthearted. Who cared if he was hung up on his ex and his mom was crazy? Clearly the pressure of the situation was getting to him.

She made sure she kept her tone playful. "Then I need gory details for several weeks' worth of dating."

He grinned and relaxed back into his chair. "Oh, I'm still on my best behavior, then. You think I'm endlessly charming. It would never occur to you that I might have faults."

She chuckled. He'd gotten a lot smoother since high school.

"I know you like food and restaurants and cooking. What else do you do for fun?

"I bake."

Too bad he had so much baggage. They actually had a lot in common. She loved eating food made by other people.

"What else?"

"Anything to do with the water. Rowing, sailing, swimming. I was on the polo team in high school. I'm on a men's rowing team now. We practice in the bay, where the water is quieter, and we compete in a regatta every spring."

"Don't you have to wake up early to row?"

Early mornings were the devil. She could think of nothing she hated so much as dragging herself out of bed when the sky was still dark.

He laughed. "Yeah. I row before work usually. I lead a team of engineers and most of my coworkers like to start work early and finish early, so they can spend time with their kids. It's easier for me to adjust my schedule to them."

"Then when you finish early, you can go home and bake."

"Exactly. Or to the gym or happy hour or out on a date with you." His voice was husky.

Her face heated. Was he flirting? Or was he just practicing his convincing-boyfriend routine?

Better to ignore it.

"Why don't you tell me about your family?"

"You've met my mom."

Ugh. I most certainly did. "What about your sister?"

"Morgan. She's the youngest, the only girl." His face turned thoughtful. "She's a social butterfly. Their wedding will be huge."

That meant there would be lots of people to convince.

Kate swallowed hard and tried to channel Beth's optimism.

"Her fiancé is Michael. He's more shy and reserved, a perfect match for my sister. It's amazing how two people can just fit together, you know?"

A wave of longing and loneliness washed over her. She'd never experienced that kind of relationship, but she knew what they looked like. Whenever Rachel walked into a room, Frank's eyes followed her, and he subconsciously mirrored her positions and posture. Had anyone ever been that in sync with her?

James focused on folding the paper wrapper for his chopsticks into smaller and smaller squares. For the briefest second, his expression turned dark.

An idea burrowed in the corner of her mind. *Is he talking about himself and Brooke?*

Kate willed her voice to sound calm and cheerful. "I know what you mean. I'm always jealous of those kinds of couples."

Jealous, yes, but that kind of happiness seemed determined to elude her. Since high school she'd never lived anywhere more than a handful of years and she had yet to meet a man worth staying in one place for. Besides, her career was the most important thing. Until that got on track, she didn't have room in her life for a relationship.

Someday maybe.

He nodded, but didn't meet her eye. "My brother and his wife are exactly the same way. Greg flies by the seat of his pants while Laurie keeps him from blowing up the house. They met in high school, at Fallston."

Opposites attract. Beth's voice echoed through her head. Like a baker and someone who's gluten intolerant. Or a morning person and a night owl. She banished the thought. *Don't be ridiculous.* To complement one another, people had to balance in more profound ways. They had to bring out important qualities in one another. Like the way Frank helped her sister stay calm when things got hectic or stressful.

A connection like that wasn't automatic. It took time to build.

She ran a shaky hand through her hair. "Where did your parents meet?

He seized her chopstick wrapper and started to fold it, too. "Fallston. Basically everyone in my family is high school sweethearts. Both sets of my grandparents met there, too."

The back of her neck tingled. How would it feel to be the only one who was still single?

"Oh." She didn't know what else to say. What had happened between him and Brooke?

She examined him. There was more to that story.

It was a good thing she'd made it clear that this was a favor between friends.

He sighed. "Needless to say, my parents are into that whole scene. All the Fallston parties and fund-raising committees. They care about image, what other people think of them." His tone was dismissive.

She stilled. "And you don't?" Why had he agreed to take her to the wedding if he didn't care what people thought?

"And I don't." He cocked an eyebrow. "What? You don't believe me?"

Her chest tightened. No, she didn't believe him. But it wasn't the kind of thing you said aloud.

"No. I'm sorry, I wasn't saying that. I just meant if that's important to the rest of your family—"

He cut her off. "I don't always have a lot in common with my family. I love them, but you know how it is."

Her spine prickled. She didn't know how it was. She only had Rachel, Frank, and the twins. Did he have any idea how lucky he was? Did he understand that a crazy, overbearing family was loads better than no family at all?

"I didn't mean to assume."

James ruffled his hair with his hand and sighed. "Don't worry about it. I'm supposed to tell you all of the gory details of my life, right?"

She summoned her warmest smile. "If you want, we can swap gory life details. It only seems fair."

His eyes lightened. "I like that plan. I'll be a gentleman and let you go first. Got anything juicy to share?"

Kate tried to think of a story that would amuse him and not make her sound like a complete dweeb. "A few months after I adopted Wally, I was backing down a steep driveway and didn't realize there was a car parked across the street. I backed into the car and got out to leave a note, but I left my car running. Wally jumped on the power locks and locked me out. I had to call the fire department to break me in. The dispatcher laughed his ass off and sent ten guys to jimmy the lock. I think they were bored and needed a good laugh. My car was in the middle of the road, blocking traffic in both lanes. And, of course, as soon as Wally got out, he ran around and gave them all kisses."

James chortled. "Seriously?"

"Seriously. It also took them a few tries to unlock the door. Every time they'd get the door unlocked, he'd get excited and jump on the power lock and lock it all over again. There were a bunch of cars sitting and watching. It was horrible."

His full, deep laugh sent chills down her spine.

"You need to tell me an embarrassing story in return. That was the deal." She leaned back from the table and crossed her arms.

He was quiet for a minute. "I had so much game in high school that I asked a complete stranger to go to junior prom with me as a favor." He didn't quite meet her gaze.

"You didn't ask me, Ainsley did."

His grin disarmed her. "Damn it. You're right. That's even worse, isn't it?"

"Hardly."

"What about your family?"

That was a short story: a mother who'd been absent most of her life, a father who'd died when she was sixteen, and her beloved sister, brother-in-law, niece, and nephew.

"Just me and my sister and her family. You remember my dad passed away." Kate hated telling people about her father's death. Her eyes burned and she fiddled with her napkin so she wouldn't have to see the pity on his face.

He'd say "I'm sorry" just so he had something to say. She'd say "That's OK" because she had to respond. It wasn't OK, but Kate had never found a better response. The whole exchange tasted stale. Sometimes she wondered if there was a secret script for loss that no one had shared with her.

He reached across the table and wrapped his hands around both of hers. Her gaze snapped up to meet his. What was he doing?

She sucked in a breath. That wasn't pity in his eyes, it was understanding. Somehow James knew there wasn't a right thing to say. He knew nothing he said would minimize the pain.

"Do you see them a lot?"

Her heart twinged. "Not as much as I'd like. I had a job in Philadelphia, but it fell through."

He gently released her hands, but continued to watch her face. "What happened?"

Something cracked inside her. He was listening. He wasn't judging.

Tears pricked the corners of her eyes and she willed them away. Kate Massie didn't cry.

"My sister's in Philadelphia. I interned for the district attorney there during the summers in law school and they'd offered me a job when I graduated. Only the economy crashed and all their funding got cut, so right before graduation they revoked the job offer. I couldn't find a job prosecuting anywhere else. Everyone had budget cuts."

She paused to swallow the lump in her throat. "I got really lucky. One of my professors knew a judge in the city who had a law clerk drop out at the last minute. So my professor pulled some strings and got me the job."

It was ironic, really. Clerkships were prestigious and hard to come by, yet she'd wanted so badly to turn it down. A clerkship meant she wasn't prosecuting, which was what she'd always pictured for herself. It was only for a year, and if the legal market didn't bounce back soon, she'd be unemployed again in twelve short months.

The muscles in her shoulders knotted. *Don't think about that now.* There was plenty of time to worry later.

"But you do want to prosecute." James's voice was low and gentle.

Her breath caught. "I do want to prosecute." When she debated in her head, she always came back to the same conclusion. She wanted to advocate for children who were the victims of abuse. She wanted to make the courtroom a safe place where they could tell their stories and fight for justice. She still dreamed of prosecuting, it just felt far out of reach lately.

The waitress returned with a long wooden boat of sushi and placed it in the center of the table.

His gray eyes remained fixed on her face, which made her insides tingle. Most guys either got bored of hearing her complain or tried to solve her problem, as if thirty minutes of their time would find her the perfect job when months of applying hadn't. Nico had even tried to get her to take a job at his dad's business. But James actually listened. Even more, he seemed to understand what she said. He wasn't focused on fixing her.

Kate tamped down the flames of longing. She couldn't be vulnerable. She couldn't give anyone else the power to hurt her.

She groped for another subject. "Why don't you tell me about Brooke?"

James choked on a piece of sushi, and Kate's face heated. *Smooth move.*

She fought the urge to squirm in her seat. "I just figure, she's going to be there and she knows you better than most people. I imagine she'll be harder for me to convince."

He did want her to convince Brooke, didn't he? Otherwise what was the point of all this?

James's eyes turned dull. "What do you want to know?"

She gulped. Here went nothing. "When did you call things off?"

"The last time? About nine months ago."

She froze, a piece of sushi midway to her mouth. They'd been broken up for only nine months and she was already engaged to someone else? Talk about moving fast.

She took her time chewing and swallowing. She shouldn't pry into his personal life any more than necessary. Even though she wanted to. "How long did you two date?"

A muscle in his jaw ticced. "Nine years."

Her jaw dropped. *Ten years.* She'd never been in a relationship that lasted longer than six months.

"On and off," he added. Rather than meet her gaze, he focused on the chopsticks in his hand.

She opened and closed her mouth a few times before she gave up and swallowed her remaining questions. This was more complicated than she'd expected.

Her stomach wrenched. *You're a fake girlfriend.* It wasn't her place to dig through his personal history and she wasn't sure she wanted to know anyway.

Kate reached across the table to touch his hand. "I'm sorry I asked. I shouldn't have pried."

James lifted his head, sighed, and put down his chopsticks. "It's just…complicated. I should warn you, though. Brooke isn't going to be happy you're at the wedding."

She gulped. Well, it wasn't as if she'd expected them to become best friends forever.

"She's…" He forced a hand through his hair. "She's…not completely balanced."

She felt the blood drain from her face. Was that code for *She's going to burn your house down while you sleep*?

He reached across the table and squeezed her fingers. "She's not crazy, that's why I normally don't bring it up. Besides, it's not my information to share. I think she should be the one to tell people. She has some anxiety issues. Social anxiety. She's shy and quiet. She gets nervous. If you met her mother, it would make sense."

"Her mother?" Her head swam. Who was Brooke's mother?

"Judy. She's my mom's best friend…well, more like her frenemy. Judy's intimidating. She makes my mom look like a teddy bear."

If he was right, Judy sounded utterly terrifying.

Her eye threatened to twitch. What had she gotten herself into? She'd known the situation was complicated, but this was some daytime talk show stuff.

He studied her carefully. "It shouldn't be a problem. I only wanted you to understand the situation. Brooke and I are still close because I help her with things. I know what makes her nervous, what sets her off. It might make her uncomfortable to see you there, and I don't want that to throw you off guard."

It might make Brooke uncomfortable? What about her, his supposed girlfriend?

Her temple pounded. This was why she didn't date. Her dating Spidey-sense was busted. It kept steering her straight into the path of trouble. James, who set her blood on fire and had unresolved feelings for his ex, was exhibit A.

She took a long gulp of water.

"What about you?" he asked.

She jumped in her chair. "Me?" What about her?

The corners of his mouth lifted as he used his chopsticks to select a piece of sushi from the platter. "We're trading life stories, right? What about your ex?"

She almost gagged. "Oh, nothing interesting. I dated a guy for a bit in law school. He wasn't my type, though, so we split up. No hard feelings, though." Kate was careful to exclude Nico's name. Fallston was a small community, and James had probably known him during high school. She didn't want to discuss Nico any more than necessary.

"What is your type, then?" His eyes glittered.

She took a deep breath. What was the harm? After all, they were friends, right? His situation was complicated and unresolved, which meant he was in no position to judge her hang-ups.

"You know how you described your brother and his wife? How two people can fit together and understand one another? That's what I want. When you can both be your own people, but you get each other and respect each other. He wanted me to be the cookie-cutter version of his perfect woman. I don't know that he ever saw me for who I am."

Her voice caught. She wanted all of those things and yet she had no idea how to get them. No matter how hard she tried, she was perpetually attracted to the wrong men.

Like James.

"And who are you?" His voice was low and husky.

Her body zinged with awareness, as if determined to prove her point.

He was just talking about his ex! He's obviously still hung up on her. What the hell is wrong with you?

She sat up a little straighter. "I'm just…me? Maybe that's the problem. Maybe I don't know who I am. How can I expect someone else to get me when I don't completely get myself?"

Another reason she shouldn't date. Now that she'd landed on her feet, with a job, she needed to sort it out.

"That's terribly self-aware and honest." His gaze bored into her as if he could see all her secrets.

She gave a shaky laugh. "See, you've already found my biggest flaw. I'm always honest, to a fault. And I know all of my shortcomings. I just try to ignore them."

She snapped her mouth shut and stared at the tablecloth.

Shut up. You've already said way too much. She hated being vulnerable. As a result, Kate exposed as much of herself as required and hid anything truly painful. For the most part she buried her vulnerabilities so well she wasn't aware of them.

"That"—he picked up his chopsticks—"is not a fault."

Her heart fluttered. "It depends on how you look at things, I suppose."

For a moment they ate their sushi in silence.

"What else do you want?" The intimacy in James's voice gave her goose bumps.

Damn him with his sexy voice and unresolved feelings for his ex. "To be happy. That shouldn't be too hard, should it? I want a job I love, to see my sister more, and to be surrounded by fabulous friends and a boyfriend who thinks I'm one hundred percent perfect the way I am."

"Isn't that what everyone wants? Passion with someone who adores you?" His eyes were deep and dark as he held her gaze. "I know I do."

Her pulse raced.

What am I doing? How had they veered so wildly off topic?

If anything, tonight's dinner proved they couldn't be anything other than friends. He disarmed her so easily. If she let him in, she wouldn't be able to protect herself. When it came to James, she wouldn't be able to keep things casual, and neither of them could offer more.

She gave a half-choked laugh. "I can't imagine why we're both still single." She lifted the napkin from her lap and folded it on the table, then placed her chopsticks on top. James inspired her stomach to do wild acrobatics. If she kept stuffing her face with sushi, she'd get a stomachache. "What does your mom have planned for us?"

On the phone he'd mentioned a family dinner.

He grimaced. "Every Thursday we have dinner together, and my mom is desperate for you to come. It's small—my parents, my brother and his wife, my sister and Michael, and me."

Her stomach settled. Good. If she kept the conversation focused on details, she'd easily make it through the rest of the night. "What about for the wedding?"

He held the last piece of sushi out to her, but she shook her head. He popped it into his mouth instead. "The hotel is on the beach. I booked you a room. You're invited to the rehearsal dinner as well."

Her mouth went dry.

"Will, um"—she gulped—"will anyone notice that we aren't in the same room?"

Her cheeks burned. She hadn't thought about this at all. She'd figured she'd just stay at her place and take a cab home.

His cheeks reddened. "No one will notice. It's one of my mother's many rules for the sake of propriety and appearances. No unmarried children sleeping in the same room under her roof, regardless of whether the roof is rented or owned."

She suppressed a snort. Was he kidding? "Wait. Your sister and her fiancé can't stay in the same bedroom yet?"

He shrugged. "Yeah, if we go on vacation or whatever, Morgan and Brooke shared a room and Michael and I shared a room."

Her breath hitched. *Brooke.* Every time he said Brooke's name, it reinforced the knowledge that nothing could happen between them. Ever. That would be the equivalent of handing him her heart to stomp all over.

He shrugged. "It's ridiculous, I know, but it works to our benefit this time. My mom prefers to be willfully ignorant. She doesn't care if we have sex, but she doesn't want to know about it. Not that I'm saying we'd be having sex…I mean, you know what I mean." His face flushed red.

Her chest ached as she struggled to hold in her laughter. "So, we're not having sex?" It was too good an opportunity to mess with him. She couldn't resist.

He dropped his gaze. "Um, do you think someone will ask?"

She bit the inside of her cheek, determined to keep her composure. "I guess it could come up with someone. Hopefully not your mother."

James's mouth dropped open as she dissolved into hysterics. Her sides heaved as waves of mirth rolled over her.

When she finally recovered herself, she winked at him. "Let's assume we're having sex and be coy about the particulars."

CHAPTER SEVEN

He stared at the computer in his office, the words on the screen blurring before his eyes.

Let's assume we're having sex and be coy about the particulars. Suddenly his pants were too tight and he shifted in his desk chair. An image of Kate arching her back while he touched her flooded his head.

Damn it. He dropped his head into his hands.

She'd agreed to do him a giant favor, as a friend. The least he could do was respect her boundaries. No matter how much he wanted to kiss her, he wouldn't take advantage of the situation. Kate was off-limits. He had to accept that.

His phone buzzed and he glanced at the screen.

Brooke. Again. What did she want now? She'd called as they were walking into the restaurant last night to ask him for her Netflix password.

He lifted the phone to his ear. "Hey."

She took a shaky breath. "Is this a bad time?"

He leaned back in the chair. "Nope. I'm at work."

"Oh. OK. How was your date last night?"

He exhaled sharply. He'd told her countless times over the last few months that he didn't want to talk about his dates with other women.

"Fine. What's up?"

She always called for a reason, never just to chat.

"I need a gallon of milk?" Brooke was scared of going to the grocery store by herself. It had started as a fear of driving at night, but over the last four years the phobia had grown to include any size of crowd and most public places.

He glanced at the clock. Eleven forty a.m. He was due for a lunch break soon. "Sure, I'll grab one and swing by. You want me to put it in the fridge?"

He still had a key to her place, in case of situations like this. Patton didn't seem to mind. Then again, Patton was out of town an awful lot.

"No. I took the day off. Migraine. I'll see you in a few." Her voice was barely louder than a whisper.

The pressure in his temple built. This was why he didn't date. For the first time in nine years he was responsible only for himself and the freedom was too intoxicating to give up.

He had pulled out a stack of papers to review when his phone rang again. The screen showed a call from his sister. He sighed. He couldn't wait for this wedding to be over. Every day brought another emergency. Between his family and Brooke, he was worn out.

"Hey, Morgan. What's going on?"

"Mom is driving me insane." Her voice was an angry whisper.

"Where are you?"

"In the bathroom at Magpie's. I'm hiding." Magpie's was his mother's favorite restaurant in the Point.

"From Mom?"

"Yes. We did my fitting, and she wants the dress taken in more. Now we're at lunch, and she's berating me about what I'm eating and how I'll be fat for the wedding."

"You've never been fat, and you'll be gorgeous in your dress. You know how crazy she gets. She doesn't mean it." Margaret always tried to harangue Morgan into a waiflike skinniness that wasn't genetically possible. Her persistence on the subject grated on his nerves.

"Why does she care if I want to eat carbs? She's not the one who has to wear the dress!"

"Agreed. If you want, I can come over and sneak you bread-sticks in the bathroom." He knew the offer would lighten her mood.

"Mom said you have a date for the wedding? A girlfriend?"

His muscles tensed. That was the real reason she'd called. "Yup."

There was a long silence.

"Do you think that's a good idea? To bring a date? You know how Brooke is."

His gut twisted. Of course he knew how Brooke was.

"I'll handle it." Bringing a date would upset Brooke, but not bringing a date would infuriate their mother. He'd chosen the lesser of two evils. Besides, Brooke's fiancé would be there to look after her. Since she'd gotten engaged, she hadn't relied on him as much. She was finally improving, much to his relief.

"James, Patton isn't coming." Ice slid down his spine. Her fiancé wouldn't be there? *Damn it.* No wonder she'd called so many times last night. She hadn't wanted the Netflix password, she'd probably wanted to fish for details about his relationship with Kate. Or she'd wanted a shoulder to cry on.

He squeezed his eyes closed and dropped his head on his desk. Just when he thought things couldn't get any worse. Brooke hated large social events. In the past she'd relied on James to help her through them, but since she'd gotten engaged, he'd been happy to forgo the job. Without Patton there, she'd need him more than usual.

No wonder Morgan was worried.

"I want the wedding to go well." Morgan's voice quavered.

His jaw clenched. "I know. That's why I agreed to run interference with Mom." He'd volunteered to keep Margaret off her back for the duration of the wedding. Someone had to fall on the sword. "Kate's coming. There's no way around it. I'm going to manage the situation and I'll make sure Brooke doesn't overreact and ruin your day, OK?

All he had to do was keep his mother calm, make sure Kate was included, and babysit Brooke. Piece of cake, once he cranked out a few clones.

She heaved a sigh. "All right. I'm not trying to be a pain. I'm just stressed."

He used his most soothing tone. "Of course you are. You're getting married. And you're dealing with our mother and Michael's mom. That would be enough to drive anyone into the madhouse."

She giggled and some of the tension eased from his body.

"Do you really like her? Kate, I mean." Morgan asked.

He didn't hesitate. "Yes." At least that wasn't a lie.

Her voice was warm. "Then I can't wait to meet her."

He found himself smiling. For some reason he couldn't wait for Kate to meet her, either.

* * *

The doorbell rang and Kate tripped over a tub of pipe cleaners as Wally woofed circles around her.

She flung the door open. Ainsley stood there, completely empty-handed. "I thought we were trying on dresses?"

"Yup." Ainsley strode into the house, pausing for a second to pet Wally on the head. "You have a computer, right?"

"Um, yes." What did that have to do with dresses?

"Great, lead me to it."

Kate took her into her bedroom. Ainsley's eyes narrowed as she studied the bare walls. So far she'd moved in a bed, a bookshelf, and a desk. She hadn't bothered to hang any pictures, since she'd only be in the room for a year. Maybe less, if by some miracle the perfect job came along.

Ainsley frowned. "After the wedding I'll come back so we can decorate and hang pictures and stuff. This is just sad."

Her face heated. It wasn't sad, it was practical, but she didn't feel like explaining that to Ainsley. Until she got the right job, her life was up in the air.

She handed over her laptop and Ainsley settled cross-legged onto the bed. "OK, let's get started. Any ideas of what you see yourself wearing?"

Kate perched next to her. The web page was filled with models in dresses. Designer names were displayed in each photo: Badgley Mischka. Carolina Herrera. Narciso Rodriguez.

Her throat tightened. "I hate to be a spoilsport, but there's no way I can afford one of those dresses." She didn't even want to look at them. They'd be gorgeous and then whatever dress she settled for would feel frumpy in comparison.

Ainsley waved a hand at her. "You're not buying one, silly."

She frowned. "Then why are we looking at them?"

"You rent them. I have an account. You choose the dress and they mail it to you. You get the dress for four days and then, when the event is over, you mail it back."

The nape of her neck prickled. "What if I mess it up?" She was clumsy.

Ainsley scrolled through the page, right-clicking to open dresses in new windows as she went along. "They have insurance. I have the plan with unlimited clothes rentals, unlimited accessory rentals, and unlimited insurance."

Kate inched closer to the computer screen. In that case looking couldn't hurt.

The options overwhelmed her. Lace, sparkles, full-length, short.

Ainsley handed the computer to her so she could type her size into the available box.

"So, are you excited for the wedding?" Kate felt Ainsley's eyes on her.

"I guess?" Better to keep it vague. Whatever weirdness was going on with James and his ex and his mother, she was determined to stay out of it. And Ainsley was James's friend.

Ainsley slid the computer back into her own lap. "It should be really fun. Everyone will be there and James is a really good dancer."

She nodded absently, trying to ignore the burning sensation in her rib cage. She was dying to interrogate Ainsley about Brooke, her relationship with James, and the breakup. Part of her wanted to know all the details and another part of her screamed to keep her nose out of it.

Ainsley was a veritable wealth of information, but it was also dangerous to ask her. Kate's interest would pique her interest and then Ainsley would probably tell James, which could only make things more complicated.

She'd made it clear that they would just be friends. She needed to stick to that.

"How about this one?" Ainsley pointed to a fitted knee-length lace dress.

Her heart pounded in her chest. "It's incredible. But I don't know how it would look on me." She wore a suit every day and in law school she'd lived in jeans. She'd been in loads of weddings, but she couldn't remember the last time she'd actually picked out a fancy dress.

Ainsley clicked to check the box on the screen. "Trust me, it will be incredible on you."

Kate swallowed hard. *No pressure.* Just hundreds of people watching her pretend to be James's girlfriend.

Ainsley enlarged another photo. "This one?"

It was a long red satin dress with an asymmetrical hem. Kate shook her head. Not her style. She was positive she couldn't pull off something that daring.

"So how was your dinner with James the other night?"

She hesitated. Unexpected? She couldn't figure out how to describe it.

"Fine. He's nice."

Ainsley looked at her and raised her eyebrows. "He's nice? As his girlfriend you'll have to do better than that. He's hot, right? And super smart and charming and witty and funny?"

Kate's face heated and she nodded. He was all those things, but she wasn't about to say them out loud.

With a sigh Ainsley turned back to the computer.

She clicked another box and snapped the laptop shut. "OK, all done. They'll be mailed here the Thursday before the wedding."

Kate blinked. What did she mean "all done"? What exactly had Ainsley picked for her?

Ainsley turned to her. "Trust me. You're going to be gorgeous. I can't wait to see the pictures of the two of you together."

She took a deep breath and tried to calm her racing heart. Ainsley was an expert in social functions and the Point. Kate had no choice but to trust her. Besides, when else would she have a chance to be dressed in designer dresses from someone's unlimited account? It was a generous offer on Ainsley's part and she wasn't about to complain.

Ainsley wouldn't dress her like Lady Gaga or Cher or the Stay Puft Marshmallow Man. This scheme had been her idea, which meant she was invested in it, too.

She stood from the bed. "Do you want a glass of wine? I have sauvignon blanc in the fridge and cabernet hanging around somewhere." Wine was a weekly staple on Beth and Kate's grocery list.

Ainsley's eyes lit. "I would really love a glass of white wine. Thank you."

The remaining tension seeped out of her. So what if she couldn't confide in Ainsley when it came to James? They could still be friends.

"Thank you for helping me with dresses."

Ainsley smiled back at her. "Thank you for letting me choose dresses for you. I love planning for this kind of thing."

Kate's stomach jumped. She wished Ainsley were going to be there, too.

She sucked in a deep breath and let it out slowly. Whatever happened with the wedding and her fake relationship was pretty much outside her control. She'd just have to strap in and enjoy the ride.

CHAPTER EIGHT

He pressed a finger to the doorbell and waited, his pulse pounding in his ears. For a second he almost didn't care that they were headed to his parents' house for dinner. Or that his parents thought they were dating. Or that Kate had agreed to the whole thing as a favor, because they were *friends*.

She opened the front door and he leaned in to hug her. Her hair smelled happy, kind of like oranges and sunshine, and she fit perfectly right underneath his chin. His chest swelled and he fought the urge to pull her closer.

He stepped away and glanced at her, careful not to let his eyes linger too long. "You look beautiful."

Beautiful didn't begin to describe it. Her black dress had a wide neck, which accented the lines of her collarbones and the hollow at the base of her throat. He longed to lean over and kiss her neck, to make her shiver as his tongue trailed over the sensitive skin.

His heart thudded in his chest. *Shit.* This was going to be a lot harder than he'd thought.

She playfully tugged at the cuff of his blue button-down shirt. "Thank you. You look rather dapper yourself."

He spun on his heel and hightailed it to the car, where he pulled open the passenger-side door. He held his hand out to her, ready to help her in.

She stopped and looked at him with her head cocked to the side. "You have really good manners. It's charming." Then she put her hand in his.

Warmth flooded him and he squeezed her fingers lightly.

One point for his mother. Manners had always been important to her and she'd drilled them into his head when he was a child. His brother Greg had been a less willing recipient.

He went around to the driver's side and climbed into the seat.

Kate smoothed her skirt. "You said you're an engineer? What kind of engineer are you?"

"Aerospace." It sounded so much cooler than it was.

She beamed. "I remember you said at prom that's what you wanted to do. That's so awesome that you did it!"

He gripped the wheel more tightly. She remembered that?

"What made you choose aerospace?"

He paused. Were you supposed to tell women you'd gone to space camp? Ainsley would vote no.

"I've always been fascinated with the way things work. When I was little I'd take all my toys apart and put them back together." There was a beat of silence. "And my parents sent me to space camp when I was ten, which started the obsession."

Sorry, Ainsley.

She let out a quick laugh. "That's awesome. It sounds like your parents are really supportive."

He tapped his thumb on the steering wheel. *Supportive* wasn't the word that came to mind when he thought of his parents.

He stiffened. Speaking of his parents, they were only a few miles from the house. He'd better make sure she was prepared. Not that you could be properly prepared for the human tornado he called Mother.

He kept his eyes glued to the road ahead. "Look, Kate, I don't know if Ainsley told you, but my mom is kind of…overwhelming."

His head pounded. *Overwhelming* didn't begin to adequately describe her.

He glanced at her. She was biting her lip and uncertainty was etched across her face. She traced a pattern on the bare part of her leg with her fingers. A fierce desire to gather her against him and kiss away her anxiety welled up inside him.

"Don't take her personally. She's like that with everyone, you'll see."

Her voice was soft. "Is that your way of telling me she isn't going to like me?"

Her words sucked the breath right out of him. This was a mistake. He couldn't subject Kate to his family. He should turn the car around and take her home, where she was safely out of his mother's reach.

Then her voice turned steely. "I guess it's a good thing I like a challenge. I'll make it my mission to get her to like me."

The tightness in his chest eased. His mother wouldn't see Kate coming. She was tougher than she looked.

He brushed his hand over hers. "If it makes you feel any better, I'm pretty sure my mom doesn't like *me*."

She giggled.

He squeezed her hand. He wouldn't put up with his mom's bullshit when it came to Kate.

He pulled into the driveway and punched the entry code into the keypad. The wrought iron gate slid open and Kate tensed beside him. "I forgot how amazing your house is."

"My parents' house." His words were sharp and clipped. Up until this year, his father's business had done well, and as a child he'd thought everyone had a maid, a cook, and an indoor-outdoor pool.

But the house had always been too big. His mother insisted she needed space to host parties, but to him it seemed a waste of money. Especially now that it was just the two of them.

She pursed her lips. "Right, your parents' house."

He pulled up behind the garage and parked. No other cars, which meant they'd beaten Greg and Morgan.

Crap. When it came to his parents, he believed in safety in numbers. Now he and Kate would have to make small talk with them. Alone. Which meant his mother would have more opportunities to interrogate her.

He slammed the driver-side door with a loud bang. Before he could walk around to the passenger side she'd hopped out on her own. Hopefully his mom wasn't watching from one of the windows.

He planted his feet and straightened his spine, steeling himself before he rang the doorbell. He reached for Kate's hand and had to remind himself not to squeeze too tightly.

Her hand was not a stress ball.

His father opened the front door, his face impassive as always. He never showed emotion.

"James. Kate." He nodded at both of them. When James stepped forward, his dad stiffly lifted his arms and patted him on the back.

Yup. That was as close as Kent Abell got to a hug.

The clacking of heels on the marble floor announced his mother's arrival.

"Kate!" She swept Kate into a perfume-scented hug. "It's so nice to see you again!" James shot her a pointed look. When he'd thrown down the gauntlet, he'd forgotten her tendency to overdo things. If she wasn't careful the forced smile would freeze onto her face permanently.

The others had better hurry so we can get dinner over with. He needed his siblings as a buffer to distract her from their parents' crazy.

His mother motioned to the formal living room. "Kate, would you like a cocktail? We have this delicious infused vodka. Small production, made in Maine."

Kent pushed past his wife to the bar. "No, no, Margaret. Kate has to have a Scotch. On the rocks. The fifty-year Scotch we ordered from Speyside arrived yesterday."

He stifled a groan of frustration. They were already trying to outdo one another, showing off their superior taste in liquor.

Kate's eyes bounced between them, as if following a Ping-

Pong match. He opened his mouth and was about to interject when the doorbell rang.

Thank God. Most adult children didn't have to ring at their parents', but it was another formality his mother insisted upon.

He strode to Kate's side but hesitated to put his arm around her. *That's what a boyfriend does, isn't it?* He settled for resting his hand on the small of her back, his palm brushing the smooth fabric of her dress. She subtly angled herself closer to him and he caught another whiff of her hair.

Her nearness filled his senses and eased the tension in his shoulders.

He tilted his head down, so his mouth was right next to her ear. "They always fight. Don't worry," he told her in a low whisper.

He ached to stay that way, the two of them folded together, but his sister's voice sliced through the air.

"Hello!" Morgan approached Kate and hugged her without hesitation. "It's really nice to meet you, Kate."

He smiled. He'd known the two of them would hit it off. Next she hugged James, squeezing him tight around his waist.

When she released him, Michael stood behind her.

"Hey, Michael." He slapped him on the back in a half hug. "This is my girlfriend, Kate."

The sentence rolled easily off his tongue, catching him by surprise. His feet were rooted to the floor as he watched Kate reach out and gently squeeze Michael's hand.

"It's nice to meet you."

Michael returned her warm smile. "You, too, Kate. I'm glad you're able to make it to the wedding."

Finally. Morgan and Michael were here. Everything would go more smoothly now.

His mother glanced at her watch and pursed her lips. "Where is Greg? He's always late. James, can you help me in the kitchen, please? We're trying out this new cook, and I don't know how I feel about the salmon. Oh, and Kent, can you go get a bottle of wine out of the cellar?" She bustled off without waiting for a response.

James glanced at Kate uneasily. Margaret didn't ask—she ordered. But he was reluctant to leave Kate alone with his family for any period of time.

She gave an encouraging nod and mouthed the word *go.*

He raised an eyebrow, but she nodded again.

He sighed and turned. His mother was the worst of the bunch. Kate would be fine with Morgan and Michael for a few minutes.

The minute he set foot in the kitchen his mother started. "She's very pretty, James. I don't know why you haven't brought her home before. It's like you're embarrassed of us or something."

He exhaled sharply. "Of course not, Mother. We can be a little overwhelming sometimes, though, don't you think?"

To her, the only point in dating was to find someone to marry. She didn't understand that just dating could be fun.

She pulled a salad bowl from the refrigerator and set it on the custom granite countertop. "This morning at the salon, Judy asked all of these questions about her, and I felt like an idiot. I had no idea what to say. I mean, I hardly know Kate. Isn't that odd, seeing how serious you two are?"

His scalp prickled. Why was she talking about Kate with Brooke's mother?

He needed a drink. "Things aren't that serious, Mother. Don't jump to conclusions."

He braced himself against the counter. If she could, his mother would get down on one knee right now and ask Kate to marry him.

She waved him away. "They're serious enough you're bringing her to your sister's wedding."

He rolled his neck on his shoulders. *Don't go for the bait.* Judy and his mother had known each other since elementary school. They'd gone to Fallston together and competed against one another for head cheerleader and prom queen. In college they'd lived in the same dorm. They'd gotten engaged within two months of each other, married within three weeks of each other, and bought houses less than a mile away from each other. They loved each other, but there'd always been a competitive undercurrent to their relationship.

"Well, she's here now, and it's none of Judy's business."

After this week he needed a vacation somewhere far away. Spending this much time with his mother turned his body into one big knot.

Maybe he could convince Kate to go with him. A repayment of the favor.

She pulled a pan out of the oven and poked at the contents with a fork. She'd never been much of a cook. "How do you tell when the salmon's done? She said all we need to do is broil it for ten minutes and *voilà*!"

James walked to the oven and took the pan from her. It looked done to him.

As soon as he set the pan on the counter, she grabbed his wrist, knotting her fingers around it.

"Judy's my best friend. I'm not going to keep big news from her. You know that." Her tone indicated, *Don't mess with me. I brought you into this world and I can take you right back out of it.*

Tension coiled in his stomach. Where were the antacids when he needed them?

He struggled to keep his tone calm.

"Considering Judy is Brooke's mom, I think it's better she not know every detail of Kate and me." *Kate and me.* His pulse pounded at the sound of the words.

Her eyebrows furrowed. "But you and Brooke are friends."

He gripped the counter so hard his knuckles turned white. How did she still not understand? He'd tried to explain mental illness to her a million times, but she insisted that Brooke should be able to conquer her anxiety and depression through pure will. After all, she and Judy had raised their five kids the same way and the rest of them were happy. Why, his mother always asked him, was Brooke so determined to be miserable?

"We are friends. Which means I care about her feelings." He nearly spit the words.

She held his gaze. "I worry she's holding you back and keeping you from moving on with your life."

James felt like a teakettle: full of steam and about to boil over. He loved Brooke, but he wasn't in love with her. It was the way he loved Morgan or Greg or Michael. Why couldn't his mother understand it'd never be simple? Brooke would always be part of his life and he'd always feel responsible for her. Walking away wasn't an option.

He pulled a pair of salad tongs from the drawer and slammed them down onto the counter. "Mom, we're not talking about this anymore. Especially not with Kate here."

"If you say so." She patted him on the shoulder as she walked past.

God, she's infuriating. He stalked out of the kitchen.

CHAPTER NINE

Kate stood in the living room, talking with Michael. Morgan and Kent had gone to the wine cellar to choose a bottle for dinner.

"With everything that's been going on with Kent's investment firm"—Michael's eyes flashed—"we've been thinking about starting our own business. It will be much smaller, of course, and it will take a while to get things off the ground."

Everything going on with Kent's investment firm? James hadn't mentioned anything. She nodded along, as if she knew what he was talking about.

"There's a noncompete agreement, so we have to be careful about recruiting clients to bring with us. We've been looking at an office space in the city, but we're considering having a satellite office over here, in the Point. There are a lot of people in this part of Belmont looking to hone their portfolios now that the economy is on the road to recovery."

An arm twined around her waist and she instinctively relaxed back into James's hard muscular body. Her heart raced. He felt so good. The way they fit together was so natural.

Heat pooled inside her and she sucked in a breath. It was all just pretend. He was putting on a show for his family and nothing else. After all, Michael was Brooke's brother.

"I was telling Kate that your dad and I are thinking of starting an investment firm."

James's body tensed against her.

"We could use a lawyer." Michael motioned toward her.

Her tongue grew thick. What? He hadn't mentioned that.

She plastered a smile on her face. "Michael, I appreciate the thought, but I'm afraid I'm not the type of lawyer you're looking for. I'm already committed to a future of being underpaid and underappreciated."

Had James told them all her clerkship was only for a year? Was Michael offering her this job out of pity? Or was he trying to tie her to Belmont for James's sake?

James's arm tightened around her and his voice came as a low rumble. "You've committed to a future of helping people. It's one of my favorite things about you."

A shiver ran down the length of her spine. He had favorite things about her? And one of them was her passion for prosecution?

Michael held up his hands. "All right, all right. I give up. I have good intentions, though. It's always nicer to work with family and since James doesn't want to join us, you'd be perfect."

His words sent her crashing back down to reality. It was all part of the act. She'd let the heat of his body against her blur the tenuous line separating fantasy and reality.

This isn't a dream. This is real life. Although lately her dreams about James had become more detailed. And explicit.

There was a thud, like a heavy door being slammed into a wall.

"We're here!" a man's voice yelled.

"Greg's late for everything, and it makes Mom nuts," James said loudly.

Greg looked disheveled in his suit when he entered the living room. He swooped in to hug her. "I also don't knock, which makes Mom nuts, but I don't care."

A blonde followed behind him, smiling broadly enough to show off her perfect white teeth.

"I'm Laurie. Greg's wife." Her blue eyes sparkled as she folded Kate into a hug.

For a split second her vision blurred. These people really liked each other. They hugged and argued about liquor and tried to start family businesses together. Was this what it was like to be part of a family?

Greg crossed the room to the bar and poured himself some whiskey on the rocks.

"Morgan and Dad are downstairs getting wine if you want some, Laurie," James offered.

She shook her head. "Thanks, but I have parent-teacher conferences all day tomorrow. I'm the designated driver tonight."

James had told her that Laurie was an elementary school teacher.

Greg took a long gulp of his drink. "Traffic was horrible. Some idiot delivery truck broke down in the left lane on Eighty-Three, and it was backed up all the way into downtown. Then a bunch of morons started driving on the shoulder, so other morons pulled their cars out to block the shoulder." Greg slung an arm over his wife's shoulders.

Heels clacked down the hall and rang through the house again.

"You're late." Margaret appeared in the doorway.

"It's lovely to see you, too, Mother." Greg gave her a peck on the cheek.

"Hello, Laurie, dear. You look beautiful." Margaret leaned in to squeeze her daughter-in-law.

"Sorry we're late, Margaret. I got stuck late at school and then traffic was horrible."

Margaret shook her head. "You let them work you too hard. The state doesn't pay you enough to stay late."

According to James, his mother was not a fan of the fact that Laurie worked for the public school system. She'd encouraged Laurie to get a job at Fallston, at least until they had a baby, but Laurie had declined.

Kate examined the smiling blonde with the friendly eyes. They were going to be friends. She could tell already.

Laurie squeezed Margaret's hand. "Thanks for worrying, but you know I love my job."

"And you're damn good at it." Greg planted a kiss on his wife's cheek.

Her stomach hollowed. How would it feel to have someone talk about her that way? Someone who meant it, not someone who was pretending for his family?

She pushed the thought aside. First she needed to get the job.

"Anyway, dinner's ready. Let's move to the dining room." Margaret made shooing motions with her hands.

Kate followed the others and stifled a smirk when she noticed place cards at each seat. *For a weekly family dinner?* She searched for her name.

She froze when she got to her place. Of course she was the lucky one seated next to the hostess.

She lowered herself into the seat and took a long sip of the wine Kent poured for her.

Margaret immediately fixed her with an intense gaze. "Where did you go to college, Kate?"

"NYU." She put a small bite of salad in her mouth and chewed.

Margaret's nose wrinkled. "That's an awfully big school in a dirty city. What took you there?"

She laughed. "The chance to be lost in an exciting city. I found Belmont to be a little…suffocating."

Margaret touched her cloth napkin to her mouth. "And law school?"

"UPenn. My sister lives in Philadelphia." She waited for Margaret's reaction. What could she say? She loved large, dirty cities. Unlike in Belmont, people didn't already know she was the girl with the dead father. It was freeing.

Margaret frowned. "I've heard that's an awfully good law

school, at least. Where are you working?"

"I'm clerking for Judge Waller. At the federal courthouse in the city."

She gave a sharp nod. "You made the right choice living in Belmont. It sounds like you've had enough of dirty, crowded city living. It's much healthier for you out here in the Point."

It was on the tip of her tongue to tell Margaret that she didn't live in the Point, but she swallowed the words. There was nothing to gain by poking the dragon. If James were really her boyfriend, wouldn't she want Margaret's approval?

That was another reason she didn't do relationships. Boyfriends had mothers and mothers had opinions.

From the other end of the table, Michael swiveled his head to look at her. "You're clerking in the federal courthouse?"

Kate nodded.

His eyes widened. "One of my friends applied over there. He said it's really competitive."

She shrugged. "Oh, I think it normally is, but someone backed out at the last minute. I got lucky."

Michael stared at her, and one side of his mouth ticced upward. "Really competitive, like you have to be in the top ten percent of your class to even be considered."

Kate's face burned and she wanted to melt into the floor. She'd worked hard at law school, because she'd seen it as her ticket to a job prosecuting. She'd found out that grades didn't get you very far in the real world.

James stared in her direction with one eyebrow raised.

Michael held his fork in midair. "I don't mean to be nosy, but I got the impression that to get a job over there you have to be in the top ten percent of your class at a top ten law school."

More blood rushed to her face. She took a large gulp of wine.

"Wait, that's a big deal, right? It means you're super smart?" Morgan put her fork down and stared at Kate.

Tears welled in her eyes. The Abells were not what she'd expected. They were so…nice. Warm. Supportive. Did James have any idea how lucky he was?

James squeezed her knee underneath the table. "The clerkship lasts for one year. Kate is going to get a job prosecuting when it ends."

That caught Margaret's attention. "Oh, in the city? My friend Mona works at the DA's office, but I've always worried her job is terribly dangerous."

Her mouth went dry. How was she supposed to answer that? *Actually, I'm hoping to move to Philadelphia next year*? It would blow their cover immediately.

"Don't worry, Kate." Laurie dimpled. "Everyone told me the same thing when I started teaching in the city, but it hasn't been as bad as people expected."

She relaxed into her chair. After the fake breakup, she hoped Laurie would still want to be friends.

She speared another forkful of salad. "I took two bar exams, so I can practice here or Pennsylvania."

"What about the rest of your family?" Margaret asked.

Kate swallowed hard. That was a loaded question.

"Mom, you remember Kate's dad passed away in high school." James intercepted it, and Kate flashed him a grateful look.

"What about your mom?" Morgan asked.

A pang shot through her rib cage. "I don't know."

Her mom had left when she was four and she hardly remembered her. Rachel said she had never been around much anyway.

"Oh." Morgan dropped her eyes. "I'm sorry. That's sad."

Something inside her hardened. She was used to being without her parents. She and Rachel got along fine without them. How could she miss a family she'd never even had?

James pushed his chair back from the table and shot his sister a look. "Morgan, why don't you help me get the fish. Then you can tell us all how the wedding planning is going."

Kate picked at the salad in front of her. Suddenly she wasn't very hungry.

James brought the first plate to his mother, then went around the table serving the women first. Despite her, a smile tugged at her lips. He really did have excellent manners.

When he was done, he and Morgan took their chairs. Nobody lifted their forks until Margaret took the first bite.

"Excellent. The new cook did a good job. Bon appétit, everyone."

For a few moments they ate with only a few murmured comments about the food. Then Margaret turned her attention to Morgan. "About the wedding. Has anyone commented on the calligraphy yet?"

Morgan shook her head. "I told you we didn't need the

more expensive calligrapher with the organic ink."

Margaret huffed. "Someone noticed the superior quality, I'm sure of it. We'll just have to wait until the wedding. People will mention it. Your generation has completely forgotten the art of small details." Margaret's mouth settled into a pinched line. "Speaking of which, you did write the thank-you notes for both of your showers already, didn't you?"

Morgan jabbed a piece of salmon with her fork. "Of course. You've reminded me five times. I even let you read them, remember?"

"Good. I ordered the thank-you notes to match the invitations and, with all the calligraphy, they weren't cheap."

"I know, Mother. You've told me." Morgan's tone was becoming shrill.

Kate fought the inclination to cringe. Suddenly she understood why James had said they'd be lucky to make it through the wedding without his sister and his mother having a blowup.

"They were very nice invitations," Laurie chimed in from the other end of the table.

Margaret dropped her fork with a clatter. "I choose to believe you have no idea how ungrateful you sound, Morgan."

Kate's temples throbbed. She shrank in on herself, wishing she could blink and be on the sofa with Beth and Wally.

"I choose to believe you have no idea how shrewish you sound, Mother." Morgan shoved her chair back from the table and stormed out of the room. The swinging door continued to flap back and forth from the force of her push.

Michael stood and moved in the direction of the kitchen.

"Oh, don't bother." Margaret waved him back to his seat. "I have to go check on dessert anyway." She followed after her daughter.

Angry voices rippled through the walls. Kate glanced around the table, but everyone else kept eating.

"Welcome to the family, Kate." Greg raised his glass in a faux toast. "This is us on our best behavior."

She giggled and James gave her a tight smile. Laurie grinned openly, while Kent chugged his martini.

Michael shrugged his shoulders. "Only one fight before dessert. That's hardly a record."

"I might as well start clearing plates if everyone's finished. I think it's better if we wrap this up sooner than later." Laurie rose from the table.

"I'll help." Kate stood.

"I've got it." When Greg stood, his long legs bumped the table. Margaret's wineglass shattered as it hit the floor.

Kate leaped from the table. She'd better clean it up before Margaret noticed. She gingerly pinched the shards between her fingers and deposited them in her cloth dinner napkin. The last piece was lodged in the corner against the threshold and she leaned forward to grab it. As she regained her balance, she heard the clack of Margaret's heels from the other side of the door.

Oh shit. Kate brought her arms close to her body, in anticipation of the impact, but the napkin slipped open as Margaret barreled through. She toppled backward as the door pushed the tip of a jagged piece of glass into her skin.

A burning sensation scorched her arm.

The breath left her body in one swoop and she nearly choked as she stared at the deep gash, the glass jutting from it, and the blood running down her arm.

She clenched her eyes shut as a rushing noise filled her ears. She was about to pass out. It had happened only once before, but she knew it was coming. She braced herself against the wall, preparing for the blankness.

A strong arm circled her waist and lifted her to her feet. She slumped against his broad shoulder and let him gently prop her in a chair.

When she opened her eyes she saw a smear of her blood on his shirt. She reached to wipe it off, but James grabbed her hand and held it in his.

"Sit still so I can look at your arm." His voice was low and steady.

Bile rose in the back of her throat. "I got blood on your shirt."

"Don't worry about that."

"I don't want to ruin the chair." Kate held her arm high so it couldn't make contact with the light-colored fabric of the seat.

James ran his thumb over her cheek, his gray eyes holding hers. "Forget the chair. Let me see your arm."

She stuck it out and averted her gaze. The memory of the glass jutting from her skin was enough to send her stomach roiling all over again. He grasped her wrist firmly and supported the rest of her arm with his other hand.

He inhaled sharply. "We need to go to the hospital."

As soon as he said the word *hospital* her throat tightened.

"I can't go to the hospital." Her voice was hoarse.

He put his hands on either side of her face and focused his gaze on her. "Kate, we're going to the hospital for you to get stitches. I'll drive you, and it won't take long. I promise. I'll stay with you."

He thinks I'm scared of stitches?

Tears burned her eyes and threatened to spill over. Desperation clawed inside her chest. "Please. I can't go. I don't care about the stitches. I just can't go to the hospital." Her voice broke. She reached out with her free hand to grab the sleeve of his shirt.

James took a deep breath. "I have everything under control. Don't worry." His left hand grazed her cheek again.

Margaret appeared with a towel. He reached for it at the same time as Kate and had to pry it from her grip.

"Trust me and let me take care of you. Close your eyes so I can get the glass out." His tone was firm.

She let her eyelids flicker shut and focused on breathing. *In and out. In and out.* Her arm throbbed.

Kate leaned forward and rested her head on his shoulder, burrowing her face close to his neck.

The room stopped spinning.

He smelled like sandalwood and apple and woods and yum.

"I watched my dad die at the hospital for months. I hate hospitals," she whispered. The words bubbled out before Kate could stop them. The hospital smell of antiseptic gave her panic attacks, but now he'd think she was silly and helpless. *What grown-ass adult is scared of the hospital?*

He tightened his grip on her shoulders. "Let's try to find one of those walk-in clinic places, then. I'll go get my car."

"I don't want to bleed in your car," Kate protested.

"Kate." He brushed her hair out of her face. "Don't argue. I'm going to take care of you whether you let me or not."

CHAPTER TEN

He eyed the speedometer and pressed his foot harder on the gas. Nine miles over the speed limit. The fastest he could go without getting pulled over.

She had to see a doctor immediately, before she lost more blood. He tore his eyes from the road in front of them long enough to glance at her.

"How are you doing?"

They'd been in the car for five minutes, and Kate was uncharacteristically silent.

"Hot. You smell good." She spoke slowly, mumbling her words. His body tensed.

He pressed the back of his right hand to her forehead.

"What're you doing?" Her voice sounded dreamy and disoriented.

"Checking your temperature."

Her skin was soft against his, but not hot. He cranked the

air conditioner and directed all the vents toward her. Only two more minutes to the clinic.

He gritted his teeth. He should have taken Kate to the hospital, but when she'd clung to him and told him about her father he'd blanked. He'd had no choice but to promise and he wouldn't go back on his word now.

He peeled into the clinic, jerked the car into a parking spot, then raced around to the passenger side.

She'd already opened the door and he reached for her.

"I can walk." She gripped the car door with her good arm for balance.

He ached to scoop her up and carry her inside, but she'd probably kick and scream the whole way.

A bead of sweat trickled down his forehead.

Just get her inside. Now.

"I'm sure you can, but you should let me help you anyway." They'd compromise. He wrapped an arm around her waist and transferred most of her weight onto him. Then he half carried, half walked her through the automatic doors.

He lowered her into the first chair he saw, taking care to place her injured arm in her lap.

Relief flooded him as he scanned the waiting room. Empty. That meant they'd see the doctor quickly.

The woman at the front desk pulled her eyes away from the TV long enough to yawn. She pushed a clipboard across the counter.

"Fill this out. They'll call you back when they're ready."

His knuckles tightened as he scanned the typed words. He didn't know half this stuff. Middle name? Date of birth?

Under "Emergency contact" he scribbled his own information.

He sat in the chair next to her. "Do you have insurance?"

"Mmmhm, in my bag." The sight of her closed eyes and pale face hit him like a punch in the gut.

He grabbed her bag off the floor and dug through it. Cell phone. Lip gloss. Notebook. Pens. Sunglasses. A mini bottle of Tabasco sauce. A screwdriver.

Why did she have a screwdriver?

He dug deeper and found her wallet buried at the bottom. He yanked her driver's license and insurance card out of their sleeves.

He scrawled the information onto the form and handed it back to the receptionist, then sat, jiggling his legs. Where was the doctor?

He focused his attention on Kate. "How are you doing?"

Kate's eyes flickered open, and he pressed his hand against her cheek to check her temperature again. It felt as if all the air had been sucked out of the room. Did they not understand this was an emergency?

"I don't feel well," she murmured.

"I know you don't." He wrapped an arm around her and she dropped her head onto his shoulder. The sight of her curled against him made his lungs constrict. *What's taking the doctor so long?*

He studied her pale, drawn face. Kate was normally confident and in control. How often did she show this vulnerable side?

He stared at the door to the examining rooms, willing it to

swing open. In another thirty seconds he'd demand immediate attention.

A nurse in scrubs stepped through. "Kate Massie?"

He jumped to his feet, then cautiously and slowly shifted her into a standing position and shuffled her after the nurse. Her body was warm and soft against his, and the orange scent of her hair filled his nose.

The nurse led them to an examining room, where he eased her onto the paper-covered table. She lay back with her eyes closed and he couldn't resist the urge to reach out and run a hand along the soft skin of her face.

What am I doing? Even like this she captivated him.

You're losing it. Tonight exemplified everything he hated about relationships: pressure, expectations, and overwhelming responsibility. He needed to remember the way his blood pressure spiked when Brooke's name flashed across his phone. He couldn't add more complication to his life.

There was a rap on the door before a doctor in a white coat entered. James studied him. They had to be kidding. His face was smooth and stubble-less and his cheeks were stuffed with baby fat. A Mickey Mouse watch ticked on his wrist.

Great. We have Doogie Howser.

"This is Kate?" The doctor peered at them through his tiny glasses. James squelched a growl and forced himself to nod.

"And you're the husband?"

He nearly jumped out of his skin. *Hardly.*

"Boyfriend." The lie rolled right off his tongue. Surely a boyfriend was important enough to earn a spot in the examining room. He'd promised Kate he'd stay with her.

"Can she sit up?"

He wrapped an arm around her waist and helped her into a sitting position, holding her upright. Her body was limp against his and he swallowed the lump in his throat.

"Why don't you put on this gown and then I'll come back and examine you in one minute?" Why did Doogie Howser have to phrase everything as a question?

James shook his head at the paper gown the doctor held out to him.

He struggled to keep his tone civil. "Can you just look at her arm? There's a lot of blood and she feels like shit. The dress is ruined anyway. I brought her here for medical help. I don't see why she needs a hospital gown." James was tempted to carry Kate right out the door and to the hospital, but he knew she'd protest. Plus she took kickboxing. Even injured he was sure she could put up one hell of a fight.

He clenched his fists and willed himself to stay calm.

The doctor eyed him up and down. *Yeah buddy, I am twice your size.* "No problem. I think we can make an exception for tonight."

He relaxed. "Thank you."

"Now, let's take a look at your arm." The doctor peeled away the towel and examined Kate's injury.

Her eyes flickered open, but she quickly averted them and buried her head in his chest. A protective urge swelled inside him as he lifted a hand to stroke her silky hair. They'd get through this. He'd get her through this.

The doctor put the towel back in place. "You're right. She needs stitches."

Why did the doctor think he'd brought her? It didn't take a medical degree to see that the cut was deep.

He'd climbed to the limit of his frustration tolerance, but Kate's warm breath through the fabric of his shirt soothed him. He tilted his head down so his chin rested on the top of her head, and inhaled the sweet scent of her hair.

The doctor stripped off his gloves and threw them into the trash can. "You should have taken her to the hospital. She needs a plastic surgeon to do the stitches."

He stilled. "Do you have a plastic surgeon here?" His voice carried a lethal edge.

"Nope." Doogie Howser reached for the door handle.

"Then I guess we aren't going to have a plastic surgeon do the stitches."

The doctor spun to face him and crossed his arms over his chest. "If I do the stitches, it'll leave a scar. If a plastic surgeon does the stitches, you'll never know they were there."

James closed his eyes and swallowed hard. The idea of Kate with a scar on her arm, because of him, sickened him. Still, he'd promised her. "We'd have to go to the hospital to see a plastic surgeon."

"Yes. They have one on call."

"We don't want to go to the hospital." James forced out the word *we*. He wanted to run straight to the hospital, but that wasn't what Kate wanted.

"Are you sure?" The doctor motioned toward Kate. "Most women don't want a visible scar…"

Kate lifted her head from James's shoulder. "I don't care about a freaking scar! Fix my arm so I can go home." Her voice was sharp.

James raised an eyebrow in his direction. Now the doctor should understand whom he was dealing with. *"Most women" my ass.*

Thirty minutes later the doctor had finished with the stitches. Before they left, James led her to the water fountain and handed her two of the pain pills.

"Swallow these."

Without hesitation she did. *She really must be sick.* He threw the bottle in her jam-packed purse and slung it over his shoulder.

"Thank you for taking care of me." She leaned into him.

His shoulders hunched.

I should have rushed you to the hospital. His parents had connections. They could have arranged for one of the best plastic surgeons in the country.

He lifted her into the passenger seat and secured the seat belt before he went around to the driver's side. He drummed his fingers on the steering wheel as he drove. Kate slept in the passenger seat as his mind replayed the night's events.

This was insanity. She'd gone so far out of her way to do him a favor and all she'd gotten in return was an armful of stitches. How could he fix this? How could he make it up to her?

He expelled a harsh breath. This was one favor that would be impossible to repay, no matter how hard he tried. The truth crashed down on him like a ton of bricks.

"Can you pull the car over?" Kate sat up, her eyes wide with panic.

Icy cold gripped his spine as he jerked the car to the side of the road. She cracked the door open and heaved into the grass.

Just when he thought things couldn't get any worse.

He ached to hit something. Instead he gathered her hair at the back of her neck and rubbed her shoulders.

"Are you OK?"

The expression she gave him was woeful. "I don't feel well."

"I know." He kept rubbing her back like an idiot. Why couldn't he think of a better way to help her?

She dropped her forehead onto the dashboard. "I'm sorry."

His spine stiffened. "*You're* sorry? I'm sorry! This has to be the worst fake date ever. In the history of the world."

"I bled on you. You had to take me to the clinic. And I almost puked in your car. I'm a total disaster."

Why would she apologize to him?

Instinctively he lifted her uninjured hand and grasped it in his. "Kate, you have nothing to be sorry for. I'm the one who's sorry. But I swear I'll make this up to you. For now let's try to get you home. Are you OK for me to drive again?"

Kate nodded, and he examined her face for a long moment before he pulled back onto the road.

When they reached her bungalow, James helped Kate out of the car and let her lean on him as he walked her to the front door. Wally's gruff bark echoed from inside and cut through the sound of crashing waves.

He knocked and Beth flung the door open. She wore footie pajamas covered in Disney characters.

"Hey! Did you lose your keys?" Her eyes raked over Kate and her jaw dropped. "Oh my gosh! What happened? Are you OK?"

Kate clung to James. "I got stitches and then I threw up."

He angled her a little closer to him, so her head rested on the upper right side of his chest.

"Oh, honey. Do you need anything?" Beth stepped out of the way and hovered as James escorted Kate through the door.

She let out a small groan. "No. I want to go to bed."

"Let's get you cleaned up in the bathroom first. Then we'll tuck you in." Beth pointed him in the right direction.

Once inside he sat Kate on the lid of the toilet. He stood by helplessly as Beth wiped her face with a washcloth and brushed her teeth.

Kate snatched the toothbrush from her friend's hand. "I can do it."

He felt his face relax into a smile. Her stubborn streak was back. That had to be a good sign.

When she was done, he helped Beth guide her to her bedroom.

Its emptiness, in comparison to the rest of the house, startled him. There was a bookshelf filled with legal volumes and brightly colored fiction covers. Only a handful of pictures hung on the walls. Her and two toddlers he assumed were the twins. Her and Beth, wearing party hats. Ryan tossing her into the surf while her dark hair whipped in the wind.

No other photos. No family mementos. As if she'd checked into an extended-stay hotel.

Beth pulled back the blue paisley comforter. "I'll help her get out of her clothes."

Her nose wrinkled as she examined the blood-spattered dress.

"I'll be in the living room." He stepped out and pulled the door closed behind him.

He paced across the cluttered room.

What if she woke up during the night? What if she threw up again? What if she had to go back to the clinic? He couldn't leave her like that. He should sleep on the sofa in case she needed him.

The door to her bedroom clicked closed.

James stopped pacing and spun to face Beth.

Her eyes were weary. "She'll be fine once she sleeps for a little bit."

He yanked the discharge papers from his pocket and held them out to her. "The doctor said to make sure she takes it easy for a few days."

She snorted. "Good luck with that. I don't know that Kate's capable of taking it easy."

What? She had to. The doctor said she needed to rest and the puking incident only reinforced the wisdom of his advice. Even if he was only twelve.

Her eyes softened. "I'm surprised she let you take her to the doctor."

She had to be kidding. "Why?"

She shrugged. "She's not good at letting other people take care of her. Probably something to do with all that time she spent taking care of her dad."

His stomach lurched. He remembered the way Kate had nuzzled into his neck and whispered that her dad had died in the hospital. He couldn't imagine what she must have gone through.

His resolve hardened. Someone needed to take care of her.

"I'm going to stay. In case she needs anything. I can sleep on the sofa if that's OK with you."

She stopped and stared at him, a slow smile spreading across her face. "You can if you want. I'm sure Wally won't mind sharing."

Good. That was settled. If he woke up early, he'd have time to go back to his apartment and shower before work. Assuming she felt well enough to be on her own by then. Maybe he should take a sick day. "I can stay with her tomorrow, too, if you need."

Beth's eyes sparkled. "I can almost promise Kate will go to work tomorrow."

His whole body went still. "She can't go to work. The doctor told her to take it easy."

Beth held her hands out, a gesture of helplessness. "You'd have to chain Kate to the bed to keep her home, but I'll do my best."

He flopped onto the sofa. "I guess you'd better show me where you keep the chains, then."

She chuckled. "I'd be grateful for the help. I don't know that I can keep her out of work on my own, even when she's injured. Don't worry about Kate too much, though. She's tougher than she looks."

He scrubbed a hand over his jaw. He knew she was tough,

but everyone needed to be taken care of once in a while.

"I'll go get you some clean sheets." She disappeared behind one of the other doors.

He pulled his phone out and checked it. Two text messages.

Brooke: Wanna see that movie? The comedy with the superheroes you mentioned the other day? It came out on DVD today and I know you wanted to see it.
Brooke: Patton's out of town, so you can stop by anytime.

He sighed. Why had she been calling so much lately? It sounded as if Patton had been traveling for work more often. Still, why was he the one she turned to? Patton couldn't be wild about the situation.

James: Thanks for the invite. I'm pretty slammed until the wedding, but I'll see you then.

He glanced to Kate's closed bedroom door. It was his fault Kate had been hurt and he was determined to take care of her, whether she wanted his help or not. It was the least he could do. As a friend.

"Clean sheets." Beth handed them to him. He could feel her examining his face. "You're a really decent guy, you know that?"

His face burned as his chest swelled. "Thank you."

She opened her mouth, as if she wanted to say more, then snapped it shut again.

"Anyway, good night." She turned and padded back to her bedroom. He watched her go, wondering what she'd held back.

He shook his head forcefully, trying to knock himself back down to earth. He couldn't let his protective instinct get the best of him. It would snowball into commitment and obligation, both of which he was determined to avoid. He and Kate were friends, nothing more. He didn't want anything more.

Did he?

CHAPTER ELEVEN

Kate stretched and looked at the clock. Nine twelve a.m. She sat up in a panic. The sheets tangled around her and her arm throbbed. She jumped out of bed and tore through the living room, searching for her phone.

Beth sat at the kitchen table ripping pages out of old books and gluing them to a piece of wood. "You're not going to work. I already called in sick for you."

She skidded to a halt. "What do you mean I'm not going to work?"

"The doctor told James you need to take it easy today and he was worried you wouldn't listen. I already called your office."

James. Her blood heated as she remembered the way he'd held her at the clinic last night, his chest warm and solid beneath her.

Her heart fluttered. He'd taken care of her. He'd told the

doctor he was her boyfriend and then he'd stayed by her side and insisted the clinic doctor do the stitches, the way she wanted. She couldn't remember the last time someone had worried over her that way. At least not a male someone.

It had almost felt real, as if he *were* her boyfriend.

A tingling sensation crawled up her spine. God help her, she trusted him.

Was she losing her mind? She dug her fingernails into the palm of her hand, willing her mind to focus. It didn't matter how she felt about him. Their arrangement was temporary. Last night didn't change the fact that he was still hung up on his ex and she would leave Belmont in less than a year. She needed to keep things in perspective.

Kate propped her good hand on her hip and pinned Beth with a look. They were nuts if they thought she was going to skip a full day of work. She needed to throw herself back into her regular life. It was the only way she could distract herself from James.

Beth met her eyes and didn't waver. "I told James you wouldn't listen, that you'd do whatever you wanted. But he was naive enough to think you'd let us take care of you."

Kate swallowed hard as she remembered his sandalwood scent, his large hands on her face, the way he'd rubbed her back and smoothed her hair.

She pushed the wave of tenderness aside. "I can take care of myself."

"I know, bunny, but sometimes the rest of us like to be useful, too. And he feels awful about last night. I think you can humor him on this one."

"What am I supposed to do all day?" She couldn't afford to take a day off. She'd only had the job for a few weeks.

"Take your medicine and relax, like a good girl." Beth placed a pill in her hand. "James left an hour ago, so he should be back soon."

Her feet rooted themselves to the spot. "What do you mean 'back'?"

Beth ripped another page from the book. "He slept on the sofa last night."

Her stomach dropped and she gaped openly. "He stayed...here?"

Beth kept her eyes on her work. "Yup. In his boxers. Which I know because I had to pee in the middle of the night. And all I have to say is damn."

Her heart stuttered. He'd slept on the sofa? In his boxers? With her in the next room? "You let him stay here?"

Her voice came out as a squeak.

The corners of Beth's mouth twitched in amusement. "Honey, there was no letting. I don't think I could have dragged him out of here. In case you didn't notice, he's about twice my height and has some seriously impressive muscles."

The mental image of him in his boxers, his strong chest naked and exposed, snapped her back to the present. "He's coming back?"

Beth stuck her tongue out of her mouth as she concentrated on attaching another piece of paper to the wood. What the hell was that thing? "Yup. And you'd better take a shower, because you look like a hot mess."

Her gaze dropped to her flannel pajama pants and button-up pajama top. They had to be Beth's. The bottoms ended at her shins, and she hadn't owned matching pajamas with cartoon characters on them since she was seven.

A sudden thought burned its way into her brain. "Who, um, who took my dress off and put me in the pajamas?"

Beth gave her a devious grin and wiggled her eyebrows. "Me, of course. But now that I've seen him, I vote you should let him be the one to strip you down next time."

She cringed.

Beth tilted her chin in Kate's direction. "You know, I saw the way he was looking at you last night…"

Kate cut her off. "Don't even think about it. You're a troublemaker."

Maybe the attraction was mutual. Maybe he was just really good at pretending. Either way, it didn't matter. They weren't really dating. If she gave in to Beth's optimism she'd get her hopes up and he'd hurt her eventually. She could tell.

Beth rolled her eyes. "Fine, don't listen to me. I'm just your best friend, what do I know?"

Kate gave her a quick hug. "I love you, too. Like you said, I should take a shower."

"Stop." Beth took a step toward the kitchen. "I have to wrap you in plastic wrap first."

Kate snorted. Was this another weird art project?

"You can't get your arm wet in the shower."

When Beth returned from the kitchen, box of plastic wrap in hand, Kate held out her arm and dutifully let Beth waterproof it. "See," she wanted to say, "I do let people help me." Although that wouldn't be enough to convince her best friend.

Beth knew her too well to be fooled that easily.

After her shower Kate used her good arm to dress herself in a pair of yoga pants and a tank top. Then she curled up on the sofa with Wally and drifted off to sleep.

A knock on the door jarred her awake.

"Coming!" she yelled. Wally followed on her heels, barking and prancing.

She yanked the door open. James, dressed in low-slung jeans and a fitted T-shirt, filled her vision. Her heart pounded.

Right. Beth said he was coming back. Somehow she hadn't quite believed it.

"Come in." Kate stepped back to let him through the doorway.

He gave her a warm smile. "I knew if I asked, you'd tell me you were fine and didn't need help, so I decided to impose my help on you without giving you a chance to shoot me down."

She tried not to smile back. He had her pegged. "Don't you have to work?"

"I took the day off." He held up the grocery bag. "Gluten-free flour. I'm going to make you my world-famous honey cupcakes." It was from Whole Foods, which she and Beth jokingly referred to as "Whole Paycheck."

"Wow. Thank you." Tears stung her eyes.

Why is he doing this? Kate couldn't remember the last time a man had done something so thoughtful for her. *Probably never.*

She wrapped her uninjured arm around her waist. "Why are you being so nice to me?" Her voice quavered in spite of her. This couldn't all be part of the charade, could it?

His Adam's apple bobbed as he swallowed. "I wanted to help." He raised a hand and brushed his knuckles against her cheek. The intensity of his gaze transfixed her. "I have a feeling you'd do the same for me."

Their eyes met for a long moment. She couldn't breathe, she just lost herself in the depths of his gray eyes.

Is this real? Or am I just high on pain-killers and imagining things?

Then she wobbled. She didn't know if it was the force of his words or the power of his gaze or the medicine, but her legs nearly gave out.

He caught her by the waist. "Careful there," he murmured.

His scent only made her pulse race faster as he guided her to the sofa.

What was happening? Had she completely lost touch with reality? They both knew what this was.

He knelt in front of her. "Are you going to be OK while I bake in the kitchen?"

Words escaped her, so she merely nodded.

He stood and walked hesitantly toward the kitchen, glancing over his shoulder at her only once.

Her heart twisted. Was she falling for him? She couldn't be. He would hurt her, she knew it in her bones.

She closed her eyes and willed the feeling to pass. She'd never lost sight of her goals for a man. She couldn't start now.

The sounds of clinking bowls and crinkling paper bags lulled her to sleep. The next thing she knew, a warm weight had settled next to her on the sofa.

She resisted the urge to lean against him and let him hold

her, the way he had the night before. What was it about him that she found so comforting?

She yawned. "Sorry I'm so sleepy." The medicine was kicking her butt, but at least her stomach had settled.

He stroked a hand over her hair, soothing her. "I want you to rest. The whole reason I came over was to force you to relax and obey doctor's orders."

She opened her eyes long enough to see that he'd figured out how to work the remote, then let her heaviness of her eyelids overtake her again.

The next time she flitted back into consciousness, his strong arms were wrapped around her and her head was nuzzled into his chest. His slow deep breathing filled her ears as his chest rose and fell beneath her. So he was asleep, too. She snuggled back into the safety of his arms, satisfaction filling her.

When she woke again, she was cold and the other end of the sofa was empty. She blinked in the light of the television and sat upright.

"Hey. How are you feeling?" Beth sat on the ottoman with a book open in front of her.

She frantically surveyed the room. He was gone? Where had he gone? "I feel OK, I guess."

She bit her lip, but the question burst out of her. "Is James still here?" Her voice sounded small.

Beth watched her carefully. "When I came home, the two of you were curled up on the sofa together. He didn't want to disturb you, but I told him you'd kill me if I let him sleep on our crappy sofa two nights in a row. I forced him to go home."

Her blood ran cold and she blinked back tears.

Why does it feel like he's abandoned me?

"You OK?" Beth examined her face.

She forced a smile. *Get it together. You're never this emotional. Ever.*

"Yeah. I think the medicine is messing with me."

Of course he'd gone. She'd slept all day, no doubt boring him to tears. He had his own life to get back to.

Beth scooted next to her on the sofa and placed a hand on Kate's knee. "How was your day?"

Her eyes were bright with expectation.

Kate's stomach cramped. He'd been nice to keep an eye on her and she'd blown it completely out of proportion. She needed to get a grip.

She shrugged. "I slept through all of it. I'm the lamest company ever."

Beth squeezed her hand. "Based on what I saw, I don't think he considers you lame."

Kate focused her gaze on the blanket and picked at a piece of lint.

"Most women would die for that whole knight-in-shining-armor routine, you know." Beth nudged her shoulder.

She pulled her knees to her chest and wrapped her good arm around them. Her voice was barely a whisper: "I really don't know." It was the truth. The more time she spent with James, the more confused she became. What exactly did James Abell want from her? And how much was she willing to give in return?

CHAPTER TWELVE

He heaved a sigh, checked his watch, and took another sip of brandy.

Across the table Greg narrowed his eyes. "What are you doing?"

What was he doing? Kate had been avoiding him all week. She hadn't been by the gym, no doubt because of her arm, and she'd responded to all his text messages with the shortest responses necessary. There had been a moment in her house when it had felt real. As she slept on the sofa, curled into his chest, he'd almost managed to convince himself it was real. Or at least that it could be.

Instead she'd barely typed five words to him all week. He'd found himself hoping she'd ask him to deliver a gallon of milk, or to rent a movie to pass the time and bring it by the house.

But he couldn't say that kind of crap to his brother.

"Nothing." He pushed the empty glass away. He'd promised to join Greg for a drink while Morgan and his mother and

Laurie fussed over some last-minute details, but all he could think about was Kate.

She was supposed to arrive at the hotel soon. The bridal party had already run through the rehearsal on the hotel's private beach. Welcome drinks would begin at six, with the rehearsal dinner to follow at seven thirty.

Greg took a sip of brandy. "You like Kate, huh?"

Of course he liked her. So what?

Greg leaned back in his chair. "Why don't you tell me about it?'

He examined his brother. Greg sucked when it came to keeping secrets.

Screw it. He could confide in Greg without blowing their cover story. Regardless of the status of their relationship, their hang-ups were most certainly real.

"I don't what's going on with us. I don't know what I want and I don't know what she wants, so I really don't have a damn clue if we want the same things."

"Huh. That sounds complicated."

He clenched the empty glass in his hand. No kidding.

His phone chimed. A text message from Kate.

Kate: Beth's about to drop me off out front. Where should I meet you?

He'd offered her a ride, but she'd declined. At least she'd agreed to text when she was close. Knowing her, she'd try to carry her bag by herself and hurt her arm all over again.

"Kate's here. I have to go meet her." He unfolded his long legs from under the table.

Greg nodded at him. "Good luck, man."

"Thanks." He threw a twenty on the table and trudged to the lobby. What was his next move? Did he say something? Kiss her? Then he risked making the whole weekend awkward. Should he wait until the wedding was over? His body went rigid. Then the next two days would be torture.

He groaned and scrubbed a hand over his face.

"James!" She stood in the middle of the lobby, a small rolling suitcase at her feet.

He pulled her into a hug, careful not to bump her arm. With a pang he remembered that she was supposed to have the stitches out soon. Would she let him take her, or would she insist on going by herself? She'd stubbornly brushed off his help the last few days.

"You're here!" Margaret's voice, followed by the clacking of her heels, echoed through the lobby. "Everyone has been asking about Kate, and I know they're all dying to meet her."

She wrapped them each in a hug.

"Why don't you two go up to your room and get changed? Everyone should be here soon and I know they're just dying to meet Kate." She winked.

A muscle in his jaw ticced. He hoped Kate knew what she was getting into. Dinner with his parents was a walk in the park compared to the chaos they were about to enter.

"I can't wait to meet everyone." Kate smiled back warmly.

His mother's eyes swept over Kate's jeans and tank top. "Oh, but you have to change. And James, why are you in shorts? Did you bring that gray suit I told you to wear? The two of you need to hurry! Cocktails have already started, and I can't make excuses for you forever."

He gripped the handle of Kate's suitcase. "We're going to change right now, Mom. I need to check Kate in first."

His mother pursed her lips. "I forgot to tell you, the hotel made an error and put you in separate rooms. I corrected it for you."

His lungs constricted. "I'm sorry, what?"

He'd promised Kate separate rooms.

His mother strode to the elevator bank and jabbed the up button with her perfectly manicured fingernail. "I fixed your rooms. You already checked in, right? You have the room across from Greg and Laurie?"

His spine stiffened. In one fell swoop his mother had zeroed in on the issue that had haunted him all week. Did Kate want this to be real, the way he did, or not?

"Mom." He struggled to keep the anger out of his voice.

Kate stopped him by pressing a hand to the front of his chest and angling her body closer.

What is she doing? Blood thundered in his ears.

"Margaret, that's sweet of you. I always sleep better when James is with me."

His mouth went dry.

"Besides—" Kate kept her hand splayed across the front of his chest. The gesture was possessive, which had him hardening below the belt. "I can't move my arm much and I need James to help me change. Give us a few minutes and we'll be right back."

Holy shit. Fire coursed through him. He wished with every inch of his being that what she'd said were true.

"We'll be back in ten minutes." Kate beamed at Margaret,

twined her hand with his, and pulled him toward the elevator.

Luckily, the elevator arrived almost immediately. He waited for the doors to close before he trusted himself to speak. "I'll fix this. After dinner I'll talk to the concierge and fix it."

He paused to rub a hand over the stubble on his chin. This was crazy, even by his mother's standards.

She fixed her large, dark eyes on him, which made his heart thud in his chest. "I'm sure it's a big bed. We can sleep on opposite sides and never touch. I'll even build a wall of pillows in the middle for you."

His nerve endings buzzed in anticipation. Kate Massie in the same bed? How was he supposed to lie beside her all night and not give in to the overwhelming need to touch her?

She gave a small smile. "Besides, I'm sure that's what everyone expects from us."

The words sent him crashing back down. He couldn't do it.

He shook his head forcefully. "No. I can't ask you to do that. We'll figure it out when we get back from dinner."

Things were already too complicated between them. He couldn't afford to make any more mistakes.

* * *

She stared at herself in the mirror.

This is just pretend.

What was wrong with her? She'd spent all week fortifying her internal defenses. When he'd offered to bring her dinner or keep her company, she'd assured him Beth was taking good care of her. Now, with only a few words from Margaret, she'd let herself slip back into fantasy.

A fantasy where she could kiss James whenever she wanted. Where his strong arms held her at night.

A tremor passed through her.

No! She was stronger than this. She needed to convince his family and the other guests, not herself, that they were dating. She tore her eyes from the bathroom mirror and unzipped the garment bag that hung from the shower curtain rod.

Besides, they weren't going to be sleeping in the same room. James had made that abundantly clear.

She shimmied into the blue lace dress.

She had to admit, Ainsley had been right about it.

The fabric skimmed over her body and showed precisely the right amount of leg. Or it would, once she got it zipped. She twisted and turned and wiggled, but couldn't reach the zipper.

Crap. She had to ask James for help.

She took a deep breath and knocked on the door leading to the room.

"I'm dressed." His deep voice sent goose bumps over her skin.

She cracked the door and poked her head through. "I hate to ask you this, but I'm stuck. I need you to zip me up. Please."

He kept his attention on the cuff link he was hooking through his button hole. "Sure."

She hesitated for only a moment before she stepped from the bathroom and spun to give him access to her back.

There was a zipping sound as his fingers skated over the fabric.

She exhaled sharply. There. It was over. She turned back to him. "Thank you. I'll be ready in one minute. I have to find my necklace first."

"You look amazing." James's voice caught as he stared at her, his eyes a vivid, brilliant gray.

Kate couldn't tear herself away from him. His gaze pierced her, suspending her in time and space.

He stepped toward her, curled his palm around the back of her neck, and lowered his mouth to hers. A delicious tingle surged through her blood and down to her toes as their lips met. He snaked his other arm around her waist and pulled her against him as his tongue swept into her mouth.

She tilted her head back and gave herself over to him, reveling in the feel of his lips against hers. His kiss turned rougher, more urgent. Her knees went weak and her head swam as she clutched him.

Her tongue tangled with his, matching him stroke for stroke. All rational thought fled her mind and she was engulfed in a cloud of James: his smell, his taste, his touch.

He pulled back for a second and his eyes glinted as he traced his thumb over her cheek. Then he tightened his grip around her waist and took the fullness of her lower lip in his mouth. A tiny moan escaped her as he sucked gently. With every stroke of his tongue, her body melted further into his. His fingers dug into her back and she could feel his heart pound through his dress shirt.

A knock sounded on the door and she stepped back abruptly, breaking the kiss.

His eyes burned with an intensity that sucked all the air

from her lungs. She shifted her gaze to the floor.

No one had ever kissed her like that.

There was another knock, followed by Greg's voice. "Little brother! I know you're in there. I brought brandy!"

James cursed under his breath and ran a hand through his hair.

"You should answer it." Her face burned. How was she supposed to go downstairs and pretend that everything was normal?

That kiss had been far from normal. It was the type of kiss she'd read about in novels and seen in movies. The type of kiss that made you see fireworks.

For the first time in her life, she understood what that meant. How had she never seen fireworks before?

Her hand trembled as she pushed him in the direction of the door.

James jerked it open, seized the glass of amber liquid from Greg, and took a giant slug. "What do you want?"

Her heart raced. What now? What did this mean for their arrangement?

Laurie's voice caught her attention. "Morgan is asking for James, and Margaret is getting impatient. I thought we'd be the lesser of two evils."

Laurie was definitely right on that count.

"We'll be down in one minute," James said tersely.

"We'll wait right here and make sure Mom doesn't send the cavalry." Greg smiled wickedly and took another sip of brandy. He planted his feet on the hall carpet, directly outside their room.

When he closed the door, James turned to her and quickly covered the distance between them. "I'm really sorry."

Kate smoothed her hands over her skirt and studied the intricacies of the lace. If she looked at him, what would she see? The kiss had been anything but fake, but what did that mean?

"Don't be sorry. We're here to celebrate your sister's wedding. We should go down and join everyone." She mustered her strongest, firmest tone of voice.

He hesitated, but she crossed the room and yanked the door open. "You volunteered to keep your mom in check, right? I have a feeling that isn't one of your brother's skills. Your sister is probably desperate to see you."

He chuckled. "I see you have us all figured out."

"Not all of you." It came out as a whisper. She caught his gaze and held it for a beat.

She hadn't begun to figure him out.

With a quick shake of the head, she broke eye contact and brushed past him to join Greg and Laurie in the hall.

When they reached the hotel bar, it was packed.

James placed his hand on the small of her back and guided her through the crowd to where his sister and Michael stood.

The tight lines around Morgan's eyes eased when she saw them. She grabbed James in a hug, then gave Kate a tight squeeze after she'd released him.

"Thank God you guys are here. They delivered the cake today instead of tomorrow and the chef is saying they don't have room for it in the refrigerator, but then I read online that if you refrigerate it, it can dry out."

Her eyes brimmed with tears and she fixed her attention on James.

He reached out and squeezed her arm. "I'll take care of it. Stop worrying and have a good time."

Next to Michael was a small woman in her fifties. The skin on her forehead was stretched unnaturally tight, a sure sign of skin treatments. "Morgan, are you going to introduce us to your friend?"

Morgan's face drained of color and her gaze flicked to James.

Kate quelled the desire to reach for his hand. She was here to support him, not vice versa. Besides, who knew what he was thinking right now? Had he seen fireworks, too?

Morgan pursed her lips. "Of course, Judy, this is Kate. Kate, this is Judy." Michael and Brooke's mother. She looked exactly like the sort of person who'd be Margaret's frenemy: slight and blond with perfect hair.

"Nice to meet you." Kate summoned her brightest smile and held out her hand. Judy glanced at it for a second, then limply shook it.

Kate bit back a smirk. Who cared what Judy thought of her?

"And this is Michael's sister, Brooke." Morgan motioned to a petite, delicate-looking blonde. She was so tiny and birdlike, Kate was almost scared to touch her for fear she'd shatter.

"It's really nice to meet you, Brooke." She shook the woman's hand, taking care not to squeeze her bony fingers too hard.

"You, too." Brooke's mousy voice barely carried over the crowd.

James leaned in and gave his ex a hug and a kiss on the cheek. "How are you doing, B?"

A lump formed in Kate's throat.

Stop that. She'd known Brooke would be here and she'd known they were still friends. She didn't have any right to be jealous.

Still, the knots in her stomach didn't budge.

Brooke twisted her tiny hands together, pulling nervously at her fingers. "Did you just get here?"

He lightly rested his fingers on the small of Kate's back. "Yeah, maybe thirty minutes ago."

Brooke's eyes remained focused on James. "Are you staying in the hotel?"

"We're on the third floor."

"At least Margaret let you stay on the same floor." Brooke smiled in understanding.

James coughed. "Actually, we're in the same room."

Brooke's face paled. There was a moment of awkward silence as she kept her gaze on James.

Then she angled her body toward him, subtly edging Kate out of the conversation. "How's the bid at work going?"

Kate's spine stiffened. Was Brooke going to ignore her all night? And was James going to let her?

"Pretty good." His eyes flickered over to Kate.

Brooke fidgeted with the belt of her dress and Kate's anger faded. This had to be as uncomfortable for her as it was for them. They were all just doing their best to get through the weekend.

"What stage of the negotiations are you in?" Brooke's voice quavered almost imperceptibly.

His fingers were stiff and wooden on her back. "The blueprints are finalized and we're working on government bidding now."

"What does Brandon think of the bid? Does he think it's going to go through?"

He cleared his throat and inched his body closer to Kate. "Yeah, I think we have a good shot."

"I can't wait for it to go through so you get your promotion." Brooke beamed at him.

Promotion? She kept the polite smile pasted to her face. A real girlfriend would know about a potential promotion, wouldn't she? Which meant…what?

"Thanks, B. It'd be nice if all my hard work paid off."

Her breath grew tight as their conversation at the sushi restaurant came flooding back. She'd known then that he was still hung up on Brooke. Why had she ignored her instincts? Why had she let him kiss her? Why had she kissed him back? What was she doing?

She nearly pinched herself. This was stupid. She didn't even want a relationship. She needed to get her head back on straight.

She spun on her heel. "I'm going to grab a glass of wine."

She walked away without waiting for either of them to respond.

She'd taken only a few steps when Margaret seized her by the elbow. "Kate! Don't you look pretty? Blue is a good color for you."

She blinked hard and tried to regain her composure. They still had two more days of this charade.

"I have someone over here I want you to meet." Margaret steered her to one end of the bar.

Kate resisted the urge to glance over her shoulder at James. They'd get through dinner, then they'd get the room situation sorted out. That was all.

Margaret pushed her toward a gray-haired woman who wore a power suit. "Mona, this is Kate Massie, Kate, this is Mona Reynolds. Mona is the deputy district attorney for juvenile and domestic court in the city."

Kate's heart fluttered. Mona had her dream job, prosecuting crimes against children. Even better, she was the head of the division.

"Nice to meet you, Kate." Mona held out her hand and she shook it. Suddenly Kate's tongue was like sandpaper in her mouth.

Margaret beamed at Mona. "I knew you'd want to meet Kate. She's an aspiring prosecutor. She's passionate about the cases involving children, like you."

Margaret put a hand on her shoulder and squeezed.

What was going on? Margaret, the ferocious mommy tornado, was networking for her? Her eyes began to burn and she shoved the swirl of emotions back down. Tonight wasn't going as she'd expected.

Mona narrowed her eyes and studied Kate. "You're sure you want to prosecute?"

Everyone had said they wanted to practice public interest law at the beginning of law school, but very few people pursued the career. The higher a student graduated in her class, the more opportunities were available to her, and the less likely she was to settle on a low-paying public service job.

She didn't hesitate for a second. "Absolutely, yes. It's the only thing I've ever wanted to do. I applied everywhere but nothing worked out."

Mona took a sip of wine. "Where did you apply?"

She sucked in a deep breath. "I was pre-hired by the Philadelphia DA, but they lost funding for the position in May."

"Anywhere else?"

Her stomach lurched. Everywhere? She'd applied for at least fifty jobs.

She gave a dry laugh. "How much time do you have? Miami, Las Vegas, Cook County, Clark County, Suffolk County, Atlanta, Memphis, Dallas, Tallahassee…um, Denver…Houston…I forget some of the others." It was almost embarrassing to list them all aloud. She'd received enough rejections to wallpaper her living room, a project Beth would have been happy to spearhead.

Mona's eyes widened. "And you went to UPenn? That's insane. I'm glad I didn't graduate into this market. What made you decide you want to do domestic cases?"

She debated for a second. She could go with the politically appropriate interview answer or she could just put it all out there.

She squared her shoulders. "Rather than walking around my whole life feeling pissed off that people do horrible things to kids and other people, I decided to channel my anger into something productive and fight for them."

Mona gave a sharp bark of laughter. "Does that mean your trial strategy is righteous indignation?"

She shrugged. "My trial strategy depends on the case. But

righteous indignation is my personal motivation." It was also one of her dominant personality traits, although she imagined it fell under the umbrella of stubbornness. That was her in one word: *stubborn*.

Mona cocked her head to the side and examined Kate for a long moment. "We've had a lot of budget cuts, too, but we're getting to the point where I'm so short-staffed I can't even run a docket." It was the same story across the country. Too many lawyers, too few jobs, and not enough money to hire them where they were needed. "Margaret will give you my card. Touch base with me next week, and I'll put you on my contact list. If we get any funding, I'll give you a call."

Her heart stuttered. Had Margaret Abell just gotten her a lead on a job as a prosecutor? After all her months of fruitless searching? Her mind raced, but she managed to stick out her hand and shake Mona's.

"Um. Thank you, Ms. Reynolds. I will definitely call you."

Margaret gave her a wink as Mona walked away. "We need to get you a glass of wine so we can toast."

Kate gaped at her, speechless.

Beth would never believe this.

CHAPTER THIRTEEN

At the first opportunity, Kate excused herself and headed for the bathroom. She couldn't wait to tell Beth her news.

The bathroom was ornate, with two rows of stalls and a sitting room. Kate went into the last stall in the second row, where she could text in peace. No one would know she was there, which meant no one would know she was being rude.

Kate: Hey. You miss me yet?

Beth: Not as much as Wally does. He's been sitting by the window whining every time a car drives by.

Kate: Poor baby. Tell him I'll be home soon.

Beth: He'll be fine. We're going to have lots of quality time. So how are things going?

She quickly recounted her conversation with Mona.

Beth: SO EXCITING!

Kate grinned so broadly it felt as if her skin would crack open. No matter what happened in her life, good or bad, Beth always made things better.

Beth: How are things going with James?

She mustered all her courage before she typed.

Kate: He kissed me.
Beth: AND?!?!?!

Her pulse raced.

Kate: I kissed him back.

She could nearly hear Beth shrieking in the quiet of their tiny house.

Beth: OMG, I'm so excited. What was it like?

The memory of his kiss seared her. There were no words for a kiss like that.

The door swung open as someone entered the bathroom. Kate dropped the phone back into her purse.

There were two sets of footsteps, then the sound of a stall door easing shut.

"He seems happy, Judy."

All the muscles in her body tightened. Ugh, Margaret's frenemy. She'd better get comfortable, because she couldn't leave until they were gone. She didn't want to risk running into them. The night was already awkward enough.

"I'm not worried about it. You know how he and B are."

Bile rose in her throat. *Shit.* She definitely shouldn't be listening to this conversation. She froze, trying to breathe as softly as possible.

Please don't let them notice me.

She lifted her feet and silently braced them against the stall door.

"They do have a complicated relationship, don't they?" The other woman's voice was high-pitched, almost nasal.

Judy gave a dramatic sigh. "You know how it is. High school sweethearts. Look at Margaret and Kent, Morgan and Michael, Laurie and Greg. James and Brooke break up, but they always get back together. They are meant to be together."

She clenched her hands in her lap and bit down on her lip. *Stay still.*

"I take it you haven't told Margaret about her calling off the engagement?"

Judy snorted. "And let her hold it over my head? No, when Brooke is ready, she'll tell James she canceled the wedding. Besides, he's here with a date. You know James. He'd never do anything that could cause a scene or lead to gossip."

Her stomach twisted painfully. She squeezed her eyes closed and willed herself to breathe.

Shit.

Crap.

Bugger.

Hell.

What was I thinking? How had she let herself get sucked into this real-life soap opera? She knew better. She'd known better at O'Riley's and at the sushi restaurant and at her house. She knew better now.

She had to put a stop to this, before it went too far. Before she put herself in a position to be hurt.

A pang shot through her ribs.

This is nothing. She knew the real pain of losing someone and she would never purposely put herself in that situation.

Her leg muscles cramped, but she didn't move until she'd heard the sound of running water, the whirr of the paper towel machine, and the swinging of the door. She counted to ten before she placed her feet on the ground, stood, and straightened her dress.

She exited the stall, washed her hands, and examined herself in the mirror. With one finger she smoothed the frown lines that had suddenly appeared on her face.

Sure, they'd shared one fantastic kiss. Sure, the chemistry between them was palpable. That didn't change things. James's situation with Brooke was obviously complicated and she still planned to leave Belmont in a year.

Delaying the inevitable would only hurt more in the end. She needed to get out there before she further fooled herself into thinking this could be real.

* * *

James scanned the bar, looking for Kate. Where had she gone? It was almost time for dinner.

He sipped the glass of soda water in his hand. He needed to be clearheaded tonight. Now that he'd kissed Kate, now that he knew there was a real chance, he had to make sure nothing went wrong. He couldn't screw this up.

He grimaced as he recalled the conversation with Brooke. It had been painful to watch her twist her hands and to hear the nervous quiver in her voice. But it had been more painful to mentally grope for ways to redirect the conversation while she ignored Kate.

Brooke hadn't meant to be rude. When it came to new people, she froze and couldn't make conversation. It was a miracle she'd walked into the packed hotel bar tonight.

So he'd stood there like an idiot, trapped between the compulsive need to help Brooke through her social anxiety and the desire to include Kate.

A memory of Kate as she maneuvered through the crowded room, radiating sexy self-assurance, flashed before him. His pulse thudded in his ears. All those years, the responsibility of being Brooke's boyfriend had nearly crushed him.

But Kate was nothing like Brooke.

He spotted her across the room and followed her with his eyes as she strode toward him. "Hey." Her voice was soft and she raised her hands, then left them in midair, as if unsure whether to touch him.

"Hey." He leaned down and kissed her slowly and gently on the mouth. Her lips met his, but she dropped her hands to her sides.

A prickle of apprehension crawled along his neck. Something was different.

"We should go in to dinner. Everyone will be waiting."

To his chagrin she bit her lip and stepped away. "Can we talk for a minute?"

His heart hammered.

Was she going to tell him the kiss had been a mistake? That she'd changed her mind?

If this was about Brooke, he could explain. Their friendship was unconventional, but he'd gradually reduced their contact over the last few months. Soon she'd be married to Patton and she wouldn't need his help anymore.

Soon he'd be free.

"James, Kate, there you are! Dinnertime. Let's move. Now." Margaret's tone was firm and insistent.

He squeezed Kate's hand and lowered his mouth close to her ear. "Believe me, I'd love to be alone with you, but duty calls. After dinner?"

Their kiss had been explosive, unlike any kiss he'd ever experienced. She'd felt it, too. He knew from the way she'd melted into him and from the small moans that had left her lips. Whatever had happened between that kiss and now, they'd figure it out. The chemistry between them was too hot to ignore.

"What part of *now* do you not understand, James Hudson Abell?" Margaret barked.

James Hudson Abell. Kate's name was noticeably absent from her rebuke.

He threaded his hand with Kate's and led her into the dining room. Apparently an accidental maiming was the key to his mother's heart.

"You're over there. With Greg and Laurie." His mother pointed.

Thank God. In the midst of a crazy family, James identified most with Greg's specific brand of crazy. Plus they were at the end of one of the long tables, which meant they wouldn't have to force any more awkward conversations. With Greg and Laurie, they could relax and be themselves.

Laurie greeted Kate with a hug. "Oh good, we get to sit with you! As transplants to the family, we have to stick together!"

Kate settled in the chair next to her and beamed back. "I'll do my best to be a good member of the transplant club. Anything I need to know?"

Laurie chuckled and shook her head. "So many things. I'll fill you in later. Bring a notepad and pen."

Laurie wasn't kidding. Dealing with his family should require a manual. Only Kate seemed to have it under control. She didn't need the manual.

Under the table James took her hand and squeezed.

The waiter made his way to their end of the table. "And what will the ladies be having?"

Laurie frowned. "I have some questions about the entrées. Do you know the cooking temperature for the pork?"

The waiter's brow furrowed. "I can't give you a specific temperature, but they do cook it all the way through."

"And the salmon, do you know if that's farm raised or if it's wild caught?"

"Wild caught in Alaska."

Laurie's frown deepened. "Then I'll go for the pork over the salmon. On the salads it says that they come with goat cheese? Is that pasteurized or, if it isn't, could you leave it off?"

He studied Laurie. When had she become such a picky eater?

"It is pasteurized, but I can do the salad without cheese if you prefer."

She nodded. "OK, then. Salad, no cheese, then pork. Thank you." She flashed him a relieved smile.

"Are your…dietary restrictions common knowledge?" Kate had a sly smirk on her lips.

Laurie blushed and looked at Greg, who grinned back at her. "Fine," she said, "you can tell them."

Greg practically bounced in his chair and his face lit with joy.

Understanding jolted through him. "Are you guys having a baby?"

"Damn it!" Greg's face fell.

He hadn't meant to ruin his brother's moment, but he'd been too excited to hold it in. "Wait! Rewind. Pretend I didn't say anything."

"OK." Greg's grin returned. He looked like a little kid on Christmas. "We're having a baby!"

Before they could offer congratulations, Laurie leaned across the table and grabbed one of his hands and one of Kate's. "But you are sworn to secrecy. I'm only eight weeks along and we don't want to steal any of Morgan's thunder. You know how your mom is."

She glanced around the room anxiously and relaxed back into her chair only when she spotted his mom at a table at least ten feet away.

She'd be jubilant when they told her. In the world of competitive mothering, this weekend was a jackpot: youngest daughter married and a grandchild on the way. That left just him.

Kate leaned forward and squeezed Laurie's hand in both of

hers. "Congratulations. It is the best news, I'm so excited for you all."

He stared at his brother, who positively glowed. Wasn't it the pregnant person who was supposed to glow?

"I'm really happy for you guys. I can't wait to meet your baby. Although I do hope it has Laurie's looks. And personality. And intelligence. And sense of humor."

He ducked as his brother sent a napkin whizzing by his head.

"Just don't mention it in the wedding toast. You don't have the best track record," Greg said.

He hunched down in his chair. He'd been Greg's best man, he'd given the worst toast of all time, and his brother would never let him forget it. He'd tried, but the words hadn't come together.

"You know how James and I are Michael's co-best men?" His brother turned to Kate. It was the familiar lead-in. "There's a very good reason for that. James can't be trusted on his own."

"Don't you dare," he growled. He should have known Greg would find an excuse to tell the story. At least now he had some ammunition. "Do you want me to keep your secret or not?"

Greg shrugged. "Not badly enough to keep this story to myself."

Laurie pointed a finger at him. "If you tell anyone our news, James Hudson Abell, I will kill you."

Funny how she sounded just like his mom when she was pissed.

He shrank under her gaze. Fine, he would let Greg tell the story.

Greg grinned and leaned back in his chair. "James hates public speaking, so he'd been procrastinating writing his speech. The night before our wedding, we all hit the bars and drank entirely too much."

It was an epic night in Abell family history. "Mom sang karaoke," James added.

Kate's eyes went wide. Specifically, his mother had sung Britney Spears's "…Baby One More Time." She vehemently denied the incident, but it still haunted him.

"Anyway, James waited until the very last minute to write his toast. There he was, at the bar at three in the morning, trying to write his speech on little index cards. He didn't read them until the next day, and right before the ceremony he was scrambling to make sense of his drunken scribbles."

Laurie rolled her eyes. "And they couldn't find Greg at all."

James snorted. "Greg was in the kitchen trying to get one of the waitstaff to tie his bow tie."

His brother lightly punched his shoulder. "I couldn't ask you, because you were busy reading drunk note cards!"

Kate grinned at their playful bickering.

"Anyway, the note cards made no sense. James panicked because there was only an hour before he had to give the speech, and he couldn't tell what they said. Of course he did what any normal person would do, which was drink to make sense of the thing you wrote when you were drunk."

James cringed. It had seemed like such a solid plan at the time.

"Somehow it wound up being a speech about the French

girl I had a crush on before I met Laurie and how, if I'd married her, our entire wedding would have been in French," Greg continued.

James had rambled and mumbled and acted, all in all, like a nervous idiot. Brooke had been humiliated on his behalf, which she'd communicated by hiding in the bathroom and crying for the rest of the night.

He sighed dramatically. "I admit it, that part was bad. But the story was about how you were meant to end up with Laurie. You know, the high school sweetheart gene. And I talked about how much I loved Laurie and how I couldn't wait for the two of you to make little non-French babies for me to spoil."

Besides, he planned to redeem himself with his toast for Morgan's wedding. He'd been working on it for months.

Kate turned to him, the corners of her mouth tugging upward. "And you said your most embarrassing memory was taking me to prom!" Her eyes danced and the tension in his shoulders eased.

"Oh please, taking you to prom was one of the best moments of his life," Greg joked.

"I knew I liked you, Greg!" She lifted her wineglass and clinked it to his beer glass in a toast.

"If we're going down the road of embarrassing stories, Greg..." He had enough material on his brother to last for days.

Laurie's eyes flashed. "I can beat you there." They all swiveled to look at her. "OK, Kate. Here it goes. The world's best Greg Abell story."

She paused for effect. "When Greg was in business school we lived in the second-floor apartment in a brownstone owned by an older Russian lady who spoke almost no English. She was nosy and she liked to come into our house and go through stuff. We caught her eating our cereal, taking our batteries, and even using our toilet. One day she walked in while Greg was in the shower."

She paused again, her face flushing red as she puffed out her cheeks. James wasn't sure she'd make it through the story before she dissolved into giggles. "Instead of walking out, like a normal person, she started to lecture him about why we should use a drain trap. Greg just stood there naked and let her yell at him in Russian."

She immediately collapsed into laughter. He glanced at Kate, who was laughing so hard that tears rolled down her cheeks.

Greg took a swig of beer and planted his elbows on the table. "Now that you guys have opened the floodgates…" Telling the landlady story was the equivalent of declaring war, and Greg had a lot of ammunition to use against James and Laurie.

"Wait, wait!" Laurie flapped her hands. "I want to hear a story about Kate. After all, we wouldn't want her to feel left out."

A delay tactic. Greg would see through it unless they distracted him quickly. James turned to Kate and brushed a strand of hair off her shoulder. "Do you want to tell the Wally story?"

His eyes fixed on the exposed skin of her neck. God, he wanted to run his tongue over it and feel her body arch against him.

He swallowed hard.

"I think I can do better than that." The corners of her mouth curved upward deviously. "Since we're telling naked shower stories."

His heart rate skyrocketed. Kate had a naked shower story, too? He loved the way she jumped into their family routine of torture and humiliation.

"In college I lived on an all-girls floor in the dorm. There was always a huge line for the showers, so one morning I snuck into the guys' bathroom one floor down since, you know, it wasn't like they were using it."

He could picture her, naked in the boys' shower, and heat blazed to his core. Under the table he clenched his hand into a fist.

Down, boy.

"I figured if I stayed quiet and waited until it was empty to sneak out, nobody would notice. I was feeling pretty confident and proud of myself until I left the shower and scared the crap out of some poor guy brushing his teeth. I hadn't realized he was there, and it caught me completely off guard. I slipped and fell and knocked myself unconscious."

Across the table Greg guffawed loudly and Laurie giggled.

"The best part was my sister's reaction. The school sent home a sanction letter that said I would be kicked out of the dorms if I had any more 'lifestyle infractions.' My sister called me and tried to do the whole parental spiel, but when I got home for Christmas break, she'd framed the letter and hung it on my bedroom wall."

By this point all four shook with laughter as they struggled to catch their breath.

"You really are accident-prone," Greg observed.

"You have no idea," Kate agreed.

"It's one of my favorite things about you." James wrapped an arm around her shoulder. She stiffened slightly at his touch and a dull throb formed in his temple. He'd almost forgotten. She'd said she had something to tell him.

He casually dropped his arm to the back of her chair. Out of the corner of his eye he spotted the waiters with the first courses on serving trays.

Good. When dinner was over they could talk. His pulse pounded in his ears. What was it she had to say to him?

CHAPTER FOURTEEN

As the waiters cleared the last of the dessert plates, an eerie calm settled over her. This was just like trying a complicated court case. You never knew exactly what was going to happen until it happened. All you could do was prepare and keep your composure.

She leaned toward James. "I'd like to talk to you. Can we find somewhere private for a few minutes?"

She hadn't been able to keep herself from stiffening when he held her hand or touched her arm, and eventually he'd given up trying.

Her chest constricted. As much as she wanted to be convincing in her role as girlfriend, she couldn't be so convincing that she fooled herself.

His gray eyes shadowed. "Sure. I need to go figure out the cake situation, but I'm sure we can talk for a minute first."

A lump formed in her throat. Would he rush off to

Brooke or would he wait until the end of the weekend? Did he know what he wanted? From watching them and listening to their families she could see that James and Brooke were still impossibly tangled together. But did James see how unusual that was? Did he know how he felt about Brooke?

She followed him through the hall and into a small meeting room.

The minute he closed the door she blurted it out. "It's going to seem weird to you that I know this, but I overheard something in the bathroom you need to know." She couldn't meet his eyes. Instead she focused on the diamond pattern in the rug. "Brooke and her fiancé aren't engaged anymore."

He reeled backward, as if he'd been hit. "What?"

She steeled herself and lifted her gaze. She kept her voice steady and calm. "Judy was talking about it. Brooke's waiting to tell you until the end of the weekend, but I didn't feel right knowing and not saying anything."

She resisted the urge to squeeze her eyes shut and pretend she was somewhere else. Anywhere else.

She took a long, slow breath. She could do this. She'd been through worse.

The muscles in his jaw worked. "Is she OK? Brooke?"

A spark of anger flashed through her. He'd kissed her not even three hours ago.

"I don't know."

His eyes glazed over and shifted to the door. "Thanks for telling me. I have to go talk to her. Will you be OK on your own for a while? Greg and Laurie said they'd be on the veranda."

She blinked at him, trying to read his expression. A sick feeling came over her.

What had she expected?

"Sure. OK, I guess." She watched him leave, then slumped into a chair.

What was he thinking? Was he off to be Brooke's knight in shining armor? And where did that leave her?

A lump wedged into her throat.

What would RBG do? She straightened her necklace and pushed herself to her feet. If he wanted Brooke back, there was nothing she could do about it.

Her chest twinged and she pushed the feeling aside.

The whole situation was like the recipe for a bad made-for-TV movie: Get a drink with the hot guy you're having sex dreams about? Check. Go to his sister's wedding as his fake girlfriend? Check. Kiss him in the hotel room? Check. Tell him his former fiancée is back on the market? Check.

She and Beth loved to watch those movies, but she definitely didn't want to star in one. Her breath hitched. Well, she'd learn from this experience.

She pushed through the door and back into the hallway, then turned in the direction of the veranda. She wasn't going to sit in the hotel room, wallowing and waiting for him. She was going to have some fun.

* * *

James watched the buttons light up as the elevator climbed floor by floor. When it reached five it pinged and the doors slid open.

He released a shaky breath and stepped into the hallway. Brooke was in room 504. If he knew her, she'd be hiding from her family and recovering from the crowd at dinner.

He knocked firmly on the door. Brooke swung it open and stared at him. She'd already changed into a bathrobe and her pale hair hung limply around her face. Underneath her eyes were dark circles. She must have covered them earlier with makeup.

His gut clenched. That meant she wasn't sleeping again. This was worse than he'd anticipated.

"Can I come in?" He shifted awkwardly on his feet.

"Yeah, sure." She stepped aside and gestured him into the room. He pulled out the desk chair and sat. She perched across from him on the bed and began to toy with the terry cloth belt.

It was a nervous gesture he'd come to know well over the years. He clenched and unclenched his jaw, then gripped the arms of his chair so hard his knuckles turned white.

"You're not marrying Patton." There, he'd said it. Better to address the subject head on.

"No." She grabbed an open bottle of wine and took a swig, then chased it with a pill. James cringed. She wasn't supposed to be drinking with the antianxiety medicine, but it wasn't his job to enforce the rules anymore. She was an adult. If she wanted to mix downers, she could.

He couldn't fix her. He'd never been able to fix her.

He'd been fooling himself to think otherwise.

The muscles in his neck tensed. "Why didn't you tell me?"

She gave a dry laugh. "What am I supposed to say, James? My life is a disaster. It has been for a long time."

There was a long, painful pause. He swallowed hard.

It was his job to tell her how great her life was and that everything would turn out fine, but he couldn't do it anymore.

For the first time in ten years he saw everything clearly. He needed to end all of this, now.

He took a deep breath.

She jumped up from the bed and began to pace. "I'm going on a wellness retreat. Somewhere in the mountains. They have a psychiatrist and a therapist and a nutritionist. They'll teach me yoga and other coping mechanisms. I won't have to deal with crowds, or people from the Point, or my mother and her expectations." Bitterness tinged her voice.

He slumped back into the office chair, relief flooding him. She was going to get help. She was going to leave Belmont. Maybe he could finally get on with his life.

A pang of guilt stabbed at him and he shook his head, trying to chase it away. Enough. Over the years his sense of guilt and responsibility for Brooke had only grown. He couldn't help her. He'd already tried his damndest.

She grabbed the wine bottle and took another long swig. "This weekend is my last hurrah, I guess. And yes, I know I'm not supposed to drink, but damn it, I have to if I'm going to make it through this weekend."

He flinched. That was fair. If the weekend was stressful for him, it had to be torture for someone with Brooke's level of social anxiety.

Especially since he was here with Kate. He jiggled his foot impatiently. *Kate.* He'd come directly upstairs to set things straight with Brooke. To make sure she knew, once and for all, that they were over. He was moving on.

His chest swelled. He was going to move on with Kate. Once he finished this conversation with Brooke, there would be no more impediments and no room for misunderstandings.

Brooke caved, her entire body folding in on itself. She wrapped her arms around her knees and sobbed into them.

James shifted to the bed and gently patted her on the back.

She lifted her face and stared at James with red-rimmed eyes. "I called it off, not Patton. It was the best decision. I can't marry him. I can't marry anybody until I get myself sorted out."

Relief crashed over him. "I'm really proud of you."

Finally. She was finally shedding the pressure from her mother, the obsession with expectations, and doing what was right for her.

She rolled her eyes to the ceiling. "Don't be. Not yet."

That sat in silence for a few minutes as Brooke sniffled and wiped her face. "So why did you really come up here?"

His blood froze. "What do you mean?"

He shifted back to the desk chair.

Brooke gave a thin-lipped smile. "Does it have to do with your girlfriend? Is she worried I'm going to try and get you back or something?"

He started. Of course not. Kate knew they were just friends.

She shrugged. "Then who sent you up here?"

His temple throbbed. Brooke hadn't looked good downstairs. He'd been worried she would overdose on her medication again. She usually had possession of enough tranquilizers to kill a herd of water buffalo.

The back of his neck prickled. How did you tell someone you cared about that you were done? She was going away. Maybe he didn't need to say anything aloud. Maybe the distance would be enough to break her dependency on him. He owed Kate more than that. For them to have a real chance, he needed to eliminate the codependent weirdness between Brooke and himself.

He swallowed. "I came on my own. I was worried about you, but also I wanted to clarify things between us. Things with Kate are..." He cleared his throat. "I think things between Kate and me could be really good. But for that to happen, you and I need to have boundaries."

He'd spent so much time panicked by the crushing responsibility of being in a relationship, when all of that stress really came down to Brooke. With Kate, things could be different, he could be truly happy.

She nodded, and her gaze dropped to her hands in her lap.

With every word it became harder to breathe. "We need to limit our contact. I'll give you your key to your apartment back. I can't run errands for you or stop by your place or go out, just the two of us, for dinner. And I can't be your first call anymore."

Kate deserved his full attention.

"OK." Her voice was barely louder than a whisper.

"Obviously, we can still do family stuff. We're related and you'll always be my friend, but we both need to move on. For real."

He held his breath as he waited for her response.

She lifted her eyes to him and he saw the tears that dripped onto her cheeks. "I know. I completely agree."

The air whooshed out of his lungs and he slumped forward. *Thank God.*

CHAPTER FIFTEEN

Kate turned left and stopped, staring at the wall in front of her. Huh. She could have sworn this was the way to the veranda. Then again, she did have a knack for getting lost.

She turned back around and examined the corridor. *Which way?* She could really use a drink right now.

Greg bounded into view from around the corner. "There you are! Where's James?" He peered past her, as if his tall, brawny brother could hide in the tiny alcove behind her.

"Talking to Brooke." She tried to keep her tone nonchalant.

"Oh." A frown flashed across his face.

Kate fidgeted with the lace of her dress.

Then Greg's expression was back to normal. "His loss, then. It's an Abell family wedding. The drinking games are about to begin, and I need a partner."

"No Margaret? No karaoke?" She followed him to an outside patio area where Morgan and Michael, Laurie, and several Abell cousins were gathered.

He guffawed. "Nah. Don't tell her you know about that story, either. She'll deny it for the rest of her life, but I was there and I can handle my alcohol better than she can. It totally happened."

She allowed herself a giggle and the churning in her stomach lessened slightly. "What are we playing? Beer pong?"

He spun on her, his jaw dropped open. "Beirut. You need to call it by the right name. "

"Maybe they call it Beirut in the Point, but in the rest of Belmont we refer to it as beer pong." She raised an eyebrow at him in challenge. She should know. She and Ryan had won the beach beer pong tournament three years in a row.

He shook his head. "Nope. You have to call it Beirut, or you can't be my partner."

She narrowed her eyes, ready to protest, but she had time to kill and nothing better to do, so she capitulated. "Fine, Beirut."

In a minute he'd see how seriously she took her beer pong.

He grinned at her. "Good. I've got to run to my car to get the cups and the Ping-Pong balls."

She stifled a laugh.

Laurie sidled up next to her and hooked her arm through Kate's. "Yes, my husband is a total frat boy."

James had said that Greg flew by the seat of his pants and Laurie kept him from blowing up the house or killing himself. The better she knew them, the more accurate his description seemed.

Kate smiled as she watched Greg walk away, car keys in hand. Would Margaret approve of college drinking games at

Morgan's chic wedding? Greg was an expert at annoying his mother.

Michael gestured to the bar inside. "I'll be right back with the beer. Gluten-free hard cider OK for you, Kate?"

Her heart twinged. He'd remembered. Margaret, Greg, Laurie, Michael, Morgan. They'd all gone out of their way to include her in the family. Soon that would be over. A heavy feeling settled in her chest.

"Kate, you want to help me move the table?" Morgan asked. At her direction Kate lifted the other side of a long wooden table. It was heavy, but they were able to move it into proper beer pong position.

A minute later Greg and Michael returned with beer, cups, and Ping-Pong balls.

"First game goes to Michael and Morgan, of course." Greg's attention shifted to her. "Kate and I will challenge. That way it'll be an even match. One girl on each team, one Abell on each team."

Kate raised an eyebrow. "What are you implying?"

He grinned at her. "You'll see in a minute. You know how to play, right? Even though you call it beer pong?"

"Of course I know how to play. What are the house rules? How many re-racks? Tell me how you Northerners do this." She squared up against Greg, challenging him.

Michael laughed. "You really get into Beirut, huh?"

She shrugged. "I'm disgustingly competitive. I apologize in advance. But Greg forced me to play, which means you can blame him for my bad behavior."

There was nothing like a good competition to distract her

from self-pity. She'd enjoy being a part of the family for as long as she could and then…her lungs constricted. Better not to think about it.

"The bride and groom should go first." She took the open package of Ping-Pong balls from Greg and handed them to Morgan.

Michael threw a ball, which whizzed past the end of the table. Morgan immediately followed, her ball hitting a cup with a satisfying plunk.

Kate grabbed the cup and sniffed. Hard cider. That meant it was hers.

Greg pulled a ball from the rinse cup and threw it, hitting the top of the triangle. Kate went next, her ball landing in the middle of the next row.

Michael groaned and rolled both balls back to them. They hit another three in a row before Greg missed.

"Shit." He glowered.

She put a hand on his shoulder. "Don't worry. We'll make it up."

He nodded grimly, then shifted his attention to the other end of the table. "Don't miss, Michael! Don't give in to all the pressure of the wedding and the family and, you know, being a husband tomorrow. It's a lot of commitment. We wouldn't want that to affect your game!"

He made her look like a good sport.

Michael shot Greg a look, then unleashed his ball. It bounced in the middle of the table and arced toward the cups. He was going for a two-pointer and she couldn't let that happen.

She leaped forward and smacked it out of the way. The ball ricocheted back in the opposite direction and nailed the cup in front of Michael, spilling beer down the front of his pants.

Shit! Her face burned.

"Oh my gosh! Are you OK? I'm so sorry!" She stood, frozen in place. If she tried to help him clean it, she'd only wind up groping him. Instead she glanced around wildly, looking for a stack of napkins.

Greg guffawed hard enough to send beer spraying out his nose. Everyone turned to look at him and before she knew it, they were all doubled over with laughter, struggling to breathe.

When he recovered, Michael turned to Kate. "What did I ever do to you?"

She covered her face with her hands and peeked between her fingers. "I'm sorry. I told you guys I'm competitive. Maybe I should put myself in time-out or something."

"No! You can't quit. We're a team!" Greg grabbed her arm and anchored her to their side of the table.

Morgan put her hands on her hips. "Ha! Greg just wants to win. Kate's the one doing all the work. He knows he'd lose without her!"

Kate's phone chimed from inside her clutch, which she'd left on a chair. An incoming text message.

Her heart leaped. Maybe it was from James. Maybe he was looking for her.

"Attacking the groom should be an automatic loss," Morgan continued.

While Morgan and Greg argued, Kate checked her phone.

Nico.

What did he want now?

She opened the message.

Nico: Didn't realize you meant James Abell when you said you were seeing someone. You know about his ex, right?

She blew out a harsh breath. She most definitely knew about his ex. Her eyes began to burn and her stomach twisted. She reached with one hand to massage the ache in her sternum, willing the momentary pain to subside, as she stared blankly at her phone.

"Earth to Kate?" Laurie approached and touched her on the shoulder, her face filled with concern. "Is everything OK?"

"Hey. Anyone know where James went? He said he'd join us as soon as he finished with the cake, but it's been more than an hour," Morgan said, her voice carrying across the patio.

Something cracked inside Kate. She bit her lip to keep it from wobbling. *Over an hour.* They must have gotten back together. Why else would he be gone so long?

She focused on Laurie's face, willing herself not to cry. "This text…it's a friend. She has a personal emergency and immediate emotional support is required." It was the first excuse that came to her head. In a louder voice she called, "I need to help my friend with something, do some damage control, if someone wants to take my spot?"

Her throat grew thick but she managed to keep the tears at bay by swallowing hard.

This is what you agreed to. She'd promised to be his pretend girlfriend and she'd suspected he planned to make his former fiancée jealous. She'd known this was what she was getting into.

But that was before. Before he'd held her on the sofa, before he'd kissed her. Things were different now.

"You sure you don't want us to wait for you?" Greg cradled the Ping-Pong ball in his hand and watched her carefully.

She gave a shaky smile. "Yup! It could be a while. I'll catch up with you all later."

Maybe. Would James even want her at the wedding anymore?

Laurie squeezed her elbow. "Let us know if you need anything."

Her eyes were full of sympathy, which only made it harder to breathe. If she didn't get out of here, she'd cry.

"Will do!" she called over her shoulder as she fled the patio. She took the stairs, to avoid running into any other wedding guests, and climbed the three floors.

She slid the key card into the door, yanked it open, and stepped into the room. She let the door slam behind her and leaned back against it.

What the hell was she supposed to do now?

Her eyes settled on her suitcase. She should probably pack and arrange for a ride home. That way she could make a quick escape when James broke the news. Or should she just go now and save them both the embarrassment?

She needed to talk to Rachel. Or Beth. One of them would know what to do. She glanced at the bedside clock. Nine thirty. Rachel was working a shift at the hospital and Beth was at a friend's art opening. That left Ryan. He wasn't the most reassuring person in the world, but he'd probably be willing to give her a ride.

"Hey," he answered on the second ring.

Kate couldn't help it. She burst into tears.

"Whoa! Whoa! What did I do now? I'm sorry! I didn't mean to make you cry!" He was silent for a moment, while she choked back another round of tears. "You're freaking me out a lot. Did somebody die? Is Wally OK? Was *The Bachelor* canceled?"

She giggled and wiped her eyes. Leave it to Ryan to put the situation in perspective. "James's ex-fiancée canceled her wedding."

"Huh?"

"James's ex is single again. He's with her now."

"And?"

Kate let out a huff of frustration. Emotional support wasn't one of Ryan's strong points. "It means they might get back together."

"Ummm…" She could tell he still wasn't following.

"I like him, you dumb ass!"

"Oh." He paused. "Oh. Shit, Kate, that sucks."

She supposed that was the best she could hope for.

"You need anything?"

"That depends. What are you doing?"

There was a female giggle in the background. "I'm on a date with Ainsley's friend."

"You're on a date and you're talking to me on the phone?"

He was hopeless.

"Yup. You're special. I made an exception just for you."

She grinned in spite of herself. Oh, Ryan. He never said the right thing, but his heart was always in the right place.

There was a clicking noise behind her as someone swiped a key card in the electronic reader. She jumped away from the door and spun to stare at it.

James. He was the only other person with a card to the room.

"Hey, I have to go. Thanks for talking to me. I hope you have a fun night."

She clicked the off button before she heard his response and dropped the phone onto the bed. Then she stood frozen, staring at the door as it eased open.

Her heart pounded in her chest. What had happened with Brooke?

* * *

He slid his key card into the slot and turned the doorknob. Kate stood on the other side, looking at him with her large brown doe eyes.

His field of vision narrowed. Kate. He drank her in, intoxicated by her dark hair and toned body. His eyes swept back to her face and froze.

His throat tightened as he took in her red-rimmed eyes and the tiny worry lines around her mouth.

He crossed the room in a few long strides and pulled her tightly against his chest.

She stiffened, then shuddered and wrapped her arms around his waist.

He bent his head, resting his chin on top of her head, inhaling her sweet scent. "I missed you."

With the words, all the tension left his body. He had missed her.

She emitted a nervous giggle. "You missed me?"

He crushed her tighter to him. "Yes."

She burrowed her head into the dip of his collarbone, right next to his shoulder. "I missed you, too."

Satisfaction pulsed through him. This was how things were supposed to be.

"What happened with Brooke?" Her voice quavered.

He stiffened. How could he begin to explain Brooke and all her issues? He didn't want to drag Kate into the mess now that he'd finally extricated himself. She didn't need the crushing responsibility of tiptoeing around Brooke, the way he and the rest of his family did.

She took a step back and wrapped her arms around herself. "Are you back together?"

He started. What? How could she think that? He'd made it clear from the beginning that things between him and Brooke were over. Today had been the final nail in the coffin of their long-dead relationship. Besides, didn't she see the way he looked at her?

He stepped toward her and cupped her face in his palms. He looked deep into her eyes. "Brooke and I are never getting back together. You have to trust me on that."

Her lips parted, but no words came out. She stared at him for a long minute before she gave a quick nod. "OK, I trust you."

His pulse thudded in his ears as he lowered his lips to hers. Slowly he teased her mouth open and their tongues tangled together.

When he'd kissed her breathless he collapsed into the armchair, pulling her into his lap. He wrapped his arms around her lithe form, cocooning her body against his.

Then he rested his forehead on hers, creating a space in the world that was for just the two of them.

"Tell me about her. Tell me what happened," Kate whispered.

His throat tightened. Then it hit him. Kate had told him about the end of Brooke's engagement, even though she thought there was a chance they would get back together. She could have hidden the truth, but instead she'd addressed it head on.

His chest swelled. She was one of the strongest people he knew. If he could do this relationship thing with anybody, it was her.

"OK." If she wanted to know, he'd tell her and trust her with the truth.

He exhaled slowly and she buried her head against his chest, twining her arms around his waist.

OK. He could do this.

CHAPTER SIXTEEN

Pounding on the door yanked her from a deep sleep.

Ugh. Kate groaned and sat up. She blinked a few times to bring the room into focus.

"Hello! Anybody in there?" She recognized the trill of Margaret's voice.

Her eyes went to the clock. Not even 8:00 a.m. She hated mornings.

She turned over, ready to prod James from the bed with a poke of her finger. His mom, his problem. But the other side was empty, his half of the sheet pulled up to the pillow.

A hazy memory came back to her of cuddling the whole night through, the warmth of his body comforting her. Then his alarm had brutally gone off hours ago and he'd planted a kiss on her forehead, tucked the covers around her, and told her he had wedding errands to attend to.

She desperately wanted to curl back into bed and let James's sandalwood scent engulf her as she drifted back to sleep.

"Hello? Kate? Are you in there?"

She threw the covers back and dragged herself to the door. She pulled it open and was greeted by Margaret's bright, smiling face.

Which quickly dropped into a frown. "Kate! Why aren't you dressed?"

She rubbed her eyes. "What?" The wedding wasn't until five. Even by Margaret's standards, nine hours left them plenty of time to prepare. Plus Kate was nonessential to the day's proceedings. Her plan was to go for a run, curl up with a book, then throw on her dress and some makeup in time for the wedding.

Margaret pushed past her into the hotel room. "The hair and makeup people are coming at ten, but in order to be ready for them we need to make sure everyone has showered first."

She put an arm around Kate's shoulders and bent closer to inspect her face. "Don't worry, dear, everyone wakes up with puffy eyes."

Kate's mouth dropped open. Had Margaret just called her eyes puffy?

"I have a serum that will work just splendidly before the makeup artists get here. Of course if I'd thought about sending you a regimen last week, but I got distracted with everything involving your arm."

She trailed off and glanced around the room. "You're not wearing your sling to the wedding, are you? I'm not sure it goes with the wedding colors and I noticed that you seemed fine without it last night."

Kate choked back a laugh. Last night she'd left the sling

in the room and wrapped her arm in a gauze bandage. She didn't think Margaret would enjoy the sight of her stitches, either.

"I'm not wearing my sling to the wedding. The doctor gave me the go-ahead to take it off."

Margaret nodded and a strange sensation crept over her. "I'm confused. I was just going to do my own hair and makeup?"

No one had said anything to the contrary.

Margaret's eyes went wide. "Oh, heavens no. It's Morgan's special day! All the women of the family will be celebrating with some pampering, and you have to be there."

Her throat thickened and words eluded her. Margaret wanted her to be with the rest of the family?

She turned her head so Margaret wouldn't see the tears gathering in the corners of her eyes.

Who could have imagined? Margaret Abell was a surprise. Kate had expected her to be domineering, overbearing, and übercritical. Yet underneath her brittle exterior, Margaret had a soft, motherly side. For whatever reason, she'd decided to take Kate under her wing.

She swallowed hard, forcing the tears away.

"Thank you. That's incredibly nice and I'd be honored to spend the day with you all. I'll probably just go for a run first, since you said everything starts at ten?"

She'd been on an exercise ban all week, doctor's orders, and she desperately needed some time to process the developments of the last twelve hours.

This weekend wasn't what she'd expected. Not that she was

complaining. She felt the corners of her mouth stretching into a silly grin.

Margaret grabbed one of her hands and squeezed. "It will be wonderful. I'm excited to introduce you to everyone. Just be sure not to run too far. And don't drink too much coffee. It's easy to get dehydrated, even if the weather is cooling off."

"Right. Yeah. Sure." By now she knew it was easier to go along with whatever Margaret said.

The moment Margaret stepped into the hall, Kate pulled on her workout gear and left for a run on the beach. When she'd finished three miles, she grabbed a triple shot of espresso and took it up to her room to drink while she showered.

The caffeine-to-exercise ratio was necessary to establish the right equilibrium.

Like preparing for battle. Kate wasn't deluded. She'd spent enough time with the Abells to know they couldn't make it through the wedding without drama and disaster. It wasn't in their nature.

She blow-dried her hair, but left her face bare. Then she slipped into a soft jersey sundress.

A brief rap sounded on the door and she pulled it open to find Laurie.

"Morning!" Laurie leaned in and gave her a hug. "I hope your friend is feeling better today. Greg wound up losing and he's pretty bitter. Morgan, however, feels validated."

Kate grabbed her purse and joined Laurie in the hallway, then followed her to the elevator.

When it reached the first floor, they wound through a maze of hallways until they reached a tearoom.

"Oh, thank God! You're finally here!" Margaret crushed them both in an embrace.

Over Margaret's shoulder Kate glanced at the clock. Nine fifty-two. *Finally?* They were early.

Margaret held a stack of papers and a clipboard.

She gave Laurie one paper and a pen. "This is the salon schedule. Laurie, you're in charge of making sure everyone is on time for their appointments."

Laurie nodded solemnly.

"Kate, you're in charge of taking attendance of the bridesmaids. Their dresses are over there." She pointed to a metal garment rack in one corner of the room. The sea of bright bubble-gum-pink satin popped out at Kate.

Kate took the list from Margaret's hand and looked down at it.

Eleven bridesmaids? That seemed like an awful lot, even for a thousand-person wedding. Laurie was accounted for, so she checked her off first.

She glanced through the room. Brooke sat in a chair, next to her mother, who glowered. She put a check mark next to Brooke's name. No way was she going over to them.

She spotted a small clump of women as they walked through the door. Might as well start there. She approached them, her warmest smile on her face.

After thirty minutes she'd spoken with everyone in the room and still couldn't find a bridesmaid named Claire.

She tugged at Laurie's elbow. "Hey, have you seen Claire? I've talked to everyone and nobody's seen her."

Laurie shrugged. "Maybe she's one of those fashionably late

people? Wait a little while before you tell Margaret. We don't want to cause a panic. Besides"—Laurie waved the salon schedule—"her hair and makeup appointments aren't for a while still."

Kate gazed about the room, which held dozens of people. The sounds of their noisy chatter buzzed around her. "Is it normally like this?"

One side of Laurie's mouth lifted into a smile. "Crazy, you mean? Margaret is like this about everything. You saw dinner the other night. Everything has to be planned in excruciating detail. Morgan isn't normally this high-strung, but I swear the two of them are feeding off one another."

Kate gulped. "Is this a normal-size wedding? For the Point?" She'd been to dozens of weddings during law school, and none of them had had this many guests or attendants.

Laurie nodded knowingly. "For Fallston, absolutely. You know how things are. Everyone is determined to outdo everyone else. *Belmont Bride* magazine will be here today. They told Margaret they were coming so it's especially important that things be perfect."

Kate sighed. "It's kind of overwhelming, isn't it?"

Laurie gave her a conspiratorial smile. "Yes. But you get used to it with Margaret."

She nodded. She was getting used to Margaret, at least a little bit.

"Hey." Laurie pointed to the door. "I think James is looking for you."

Kate's heart hammered as she turned. She met his gray eyes

and held them, the air between them practically vibrating. He raised a hand to motion her over and gave one of his sexy, lazy smiles.

Her lungs tightened.

His eyes followed her as she crossed the room. It felt as if she were floating, as if her feet were detached from the rest of her body.

She trembled as she remembered the way he'd wrapped her in his strong arms last night and held her. They hadn't done anything else. He'd just held her, and she'd reveled in the feeling. The doubts she'd had about him and Brooke had evaporated. The two of them were free to be together.

Whoa there. The thought jolted her back to reality. She couldn't get carried away. Who knew what would happen in the future?

She fingered the fabric of her sundress, her steps slowing slightly. For now she should just enjoy James. She'd figure the rest out as she went along.

* * *

He watched Kate as she crossed the floor, his attention fixed on her long, tan legs and the slight sway of her hips.

His mouth went dry. When he'd woken this morning, it had been agony to untangle himself from her and leave the room. They'd been apart only a few hours and already he couldn't wait to touch her.

He held the door open for her. As she walked through, she lifted her hand to touch his shoulder. He inhaled deeply, breathing in her clean orange-sunshine scent, and his heart thudded in his chest.

She paused in the middle of the quiet hallway and turned her dark eyes on him. He crossed the distance between them in a few long strides, then cupped her face in his hands.

His breathing was ragged as he stared into her eyes. He lifted his hand and ran his thumb over her cheekbones and her full lips. Their lush softness made him groan as he hardened below the belt.

He ducked his head and tenderly brushed his lips across hers. She parted her lips and dipped her tongue into his mouth, stroking and teasing. His hands involuntarily traveled from her face to twine in her hair.

He'd waited all morning to kiss her.

She wound her hands around his neck and allowed him to push her back against the wall. His pulse throbbed as he wrapped his hands around her hips and pulled her pelvis into him. Heat blazed through his body, pooling in his groin. He was so hard it physically hurt and he wished they could go back to the room, lock the door, and ignore everyone else for the day. It would be just the two of them, exploring one another. She turned her head to nip at his earlobe, her lips brushing against the side of his neck.

He groaned. "You're going to destroy me." The words sounded half-strangled.

He let his hands travel the length of her body, tracing her curves.

"You have no idea," she murmured in his ear.

"Is that a threat or a promise?" He rocked against her and she mewled, her fingers digging into his shoulders.

Behind them the hinges of the door squeaked and he jumped backward. She quickly tugged the hem of her dress straight with one hand and pushed her hair off her face with the other.

He turned to the door.

A snort of laughter burst out of him. It was his mother, her eyes wide with horror.

Beside him Kate raised her hand to her mouth and tried unsuccessfully to stifle a giggle.

Margaret pinched her lips together before she carefully arranged her mouth into a smile.

"Oh, Kate! I've been looking for you!"

Kate's eyes danced with suppressed laughter. "You found me!"

His mother's face turned tomato red. In a few seconds, he was going to lose it.

"Yes, well," Margaret spluttered. "We're missing a bridesmaid. Claire." Her gaze shifted back and forth between the two of them, as if uncertain whom to fix with a death glare. "I wanted to talk to you about it."

Kate rushed forward. "Of course, I'm really sorry. I noticed she was missing, but I thought I'd wait to make sure she wasn't just late. I didn't want to cause panic."

Margaret gave a sharp sigh. "She has food poisoning, apparently. Her mother just called me." That was Fallston code for *I drank too much last night and can't scrape myself off the bathroom floor.*

Morgan will freak out. His mother's icy tone indicated she was livid with the missing bridesmaid.

Kate touched his mother's shoulder. "How can I help?"

Gratitude surged through him. By now she knew what she was getting into.

His mother gave a small smile. "That's why I came to look for you, dear. We need to brainstorm and see if we can find another bridesmaid. I haven't told Morgan yet. I'd rather wait until we have a replacement lined up."

"Can you just go with ten bridesmaids?"

His mother shook her head emphatically. "No. *Belmont Bride* will be here and then everyone will see the lopsided numbers in the magazine. People will think there's a reason for it, like Morgan couldn't find eleven people to stand up for her."

He quashed the urge to roll his eyes. He doubted anyone would notice, much less care. Except for people like his mom and Judy and their friends.

His mom pressed her lips together. "We need to find a replacement who will look good in the dress. We don't have time for alterations."

"OK, I'll be right in." Kate gave him a long look over her shoulder.

His pulse pounded. Just one more kiss, then he could let her go. In a few hours this would all be over and he'd have her to himself.

"I need a minute with Kate, Mom."

She glared at him, her eyes ice-cold. "I can't imagine that you need Kate more than your sister does right now."

He sighed wearily.

Just a few more hours.

Kate smirked at him and mouthed the word *sorry*. "I'll help your mom and then I'll find you later."

He watched her retreating back. He couldn't wait to be alone with her.

CHAPTER SEVENTEEN

Inside the tearoom Morgan sat on a chair crying openly. She dabbed her face with tissues as people gathered around her. From what Kate could hear, her friends were adding fuel to the fire.

"Poor Morgan, what are you going to do? And with the pictures going in the magazine and everything!" one said.

"I can't believe she'd bail on you like this! How ungrateful. And after everything we did for her wedding!" another added.

Margaret gripped Kate's arm, her fingernails digging into her skin. "Look at her! There isn't enough makeup in the world to fix red eyes and a blotchy face!"

Kate pushed her way through the group and crouched next to Morgan. As far as she was concerned, Margaret had given her carte blanche to take control of the situation.

"Hey, sweetie, how're you doing?"

Morgan raised her tearstained face. "This is a disaster!"

"It'll be fine. You have all of us to help you find a solution." Kate squeezed her hand. "Besides, nobody is going to be paying attention to anyone but you and Michael."

This made the corners of Morgan's mouth lift a little. Taking a cue from Kate, Laurie also pushed her way forward.

"Your dress is so gorgeous, nobody will even be looking at Michael."

This earned them a bigger smile.

Margaret's shrill voice broke the moment of calm. "We need another bridesmaid! Rack your brain, Morgan. Think of someone appropriate!"

Kate huffed and sank back on her heels. *Way to make it worse, Margaret.*

"I think you can use ten bridesmaids and nobody will notice." So what if Margaret had vetoed the idea? Morgan's opinion was the one that mattered.

Margaret's strident voice rang out from behind her. "Now, Kate, I told you. Uneven numbers simply aren't done around here. Everyone will notice and it will be the only thing people talk about."

For a moment Kate was tempted to strangle her.

Margaret approached and bowed her head close to theirs. When she spoke her voice was almost a whisper. "What about Kate?"

Her eyes sparked with mischief. All too late Kate realized it was a trap. Even before Margaret had tracked her into the hall, this had been her plan.

She closed her eyes and silently prayed that Margaret hadn't food-poisoned Claire on purpose.

Margaret wouldn't do something like that. Would she?

Morgan's face lit up. "Oh my gosh. Kate, would you?"

She swallowed hard and mentally groped for an excuse. She and James had been dating for only a day. What would he think if she showed up at his sister's wedding as a bridesmaid? Her temple pounded. That was serious. A lot more serious than she wanted to be.

"Um, I guess I could try the dress on." Hopefully, it wouldn't fit. Then she wouldn't have to create an excuse. She'd be automatically disqualified.

Margaret beamed. "Good! Now that we've solved that problem, I'm off to help the florists with the centerpieces. I can't wait to see all three of you beautiful girls when the stylists are done with you."

Kate watched her retreating back, speechless. What the hell had just happened?

"Hopefully, it fits." Laurie handed her the dress. She ducked into a nearby bathroom to change.

Kate stepped into the dress, settled it around herself, and zipped the back, but she still swam in the fabric. The top was far too big for her frame. Now Morgan would have to pick a more appropriate bridesmaid.

To her surprise, disappointment stabbed at her. *I can't wait to see all three of you beautiful girls.* Margaret had included her.

She hesitated, staring into the mirror. She tilted her head to the side as she reached around back and grabbed a fistful of fabric.

It was a simple enough alteration. Beth could have done it in her sleep.

She kept hold of the fabric as she stepped from the bathroom.

Morgan's face lit up. "It fits!"

Kate bit her lip. "Not exactly. But if you give me an hour, some double-sided sticky tape, a pair of scissors, and a needle and thread, it will fit. You might not want to tell your mom I hacked it up and put it back together."

Laurie's eyes went wide and Morgan's mouth dropped open.

Her stomach twisted. Was this a good idea after all?

"Are you sure that will work?" Laurie flipped over the satin fabric and fingered the seam.

"Yes, I'm sure." Thanks to Beth, Kate knew how to sew. She'd have to sew by hand, which meant the stitches wouldn't be very sturdy. But her alterations would be fine for one night, provided she didn't make any sudden movements.

A sly grin crossed Morgan's face. "Do it. We won't tell my mom."

Within thirty minutes she'd ripped out the seams and re-sewn them. It wasn't a professional job by any means, but with some strategically placed double-sided sticky tape, it would pass muster. She prayed Margaret wouldn't examine her too closely.

"I can't believe you fixed it!" Morgan's glowing face reassured Kate she'd made the right decision.

What was it about the Abells? They consistently drew her further into their web of dysfunction and yet she liked it.

Maybe she was as crazy as the rest of them.

* * *

James and the other groomsmen lined up at the front of the aisle and waited for the ceremony to begin. Behind them the surf crashed against the sand. He shaded his eyes from the glare of the sun and looked up at the archway made entirely of white flowers. Underneath it stood a minister, clad in a simple robe and a clerical collar, holding a Bible under one arm.

He inhaled the salty sea air and closed his eyes, letting the sun warm his face. Every day in Belmont was gorgeous, but today was especially perfect.

The clear notes of a violin reverberated and he opened his eyes. His gaze fixed on the head of the makeshift aisle the hotel staff had laid out in the sand. In a few minutes his sister would walk down it.

The rest of the string quartet joined in and the first of the bridesmaids began to walk down the aisle. He let his eyes stray over the crowd, searching for Kate. He wondered what she'd be wearing tonight and hoped it would involve her bare neck. There was something distinctly erotic about the arch of her collarbones and the curve of her strong shoulders.

Something sharp jabbed him in the middle of his back.

"Ouch!" he whispered.

Greg leaned closer to him. "Isn't that Kate?"

"Huh?" Once again he combed through the crowd. There were too damn many people here. It was more of a circus than a wedding.

Greg jerked his head. "Walking down the aisle."

His throat grew tight and his eyes shot to the aisle.

Kate wore a bubble-gum-pink dress like everyone else, her hair swept to one side. His heart thudded in his chest. Her neck and shoulders were bare, and he imagined trailing his fingers across the soft, creamy expanse of skin. His body shuddered with desire.

Wait! Why was she dressed as a bridesmaid? Cold slid down his spine. Of course. That had been his mother's plan all along.

The pressure built in his temple and the muscles in his neck knotted.

Shit. Talk about pressure. If his mother had her way, he'd be down on one knee at the reception. His jaw clenched.

She met his eyes, flashed him a wavering smile, and raised an eyebrow.

He let out a long breath. It wasn't her fault. She knew his mother, but she didn't truly know his mother.

He smiled back. She was gorgeous and in a few hours this would all be over. Then it would be the two of them alone, together, at last. Kate wasn't the type of woman to suffocate him with expectations and responsibilities. She'd already shown him that. He'd be free to date her without his mother's constant interference.

The music swelled and he tore his gaze from Kate to see his sister walk down the aisle. She beamed at Michael, who beamed back. His father had to trot to keep up with her as she practically dragged him to Michael. When they reached him, she stopped and turned to her father, who lifted the veil and kissed her on the cheek.

Then he shook Michael's hand. James watched his father's face carefully. He could have sworn he saw a tear in his dad's eye.

Impossible. When it came to anything other than business, his father was an emotionless robot. And when it came to business, the only emotion he showed was rage. As on the time his head had nearly exploded when he found out Kip Davidson planned to force him out of the firm, so he could make his son Nico a partner.

He forced the thought aside. Today was a happy day.

The minister's voice droned into the microphone, pulling his attention back to the ceremony. "True love is the greatest happiness we have in life and marriage vows are the sacred declaration of true love."

The ceremony flew by.

When it came time to exchange rings, James stepped next to Michael and pressed the diamond-and-gold band into his hand. When it came to best man duties, everyone had agreed he was better qualified than Greg to keep hold of the ring.

Michael slid the ring onto Morgan's finger, to thunderous applause.

Morgan's maid of honor was her best friend from Fallston, Tippy. She stepped forward and handed Morgan Michael's ring. Then Morgan slid it onto his finger.

"I now pronounce you husband and wife," the minister intoned. The crowd erupted with another round of applause. His sister's face flushed as Michael stepped forward to kiss her.

The string quartet struck the first few notes of the recessional, and Morgan and Michael smiled triumphantly as they started up the aisle.

A few pairs of attendants followed and James kept his attention fixed on the crowd. His throat tightened and he swallowed hard. It was an insane number of people. In an hour he had to make a toast in front of all of them.

He clenched his hands by his sides. He could do this. He'd prepared meticulously. He'd pretend it was just him, Morgan, and Michael. And maybe Kate.

Still, the lump wouldn't budge.

Greg stepped into the aisle and held out his arm for Laurie, who took it with a smile. Then James walked to the aisle and waited for Kate. He tucked her arm close to his body and leaned so his mouth was next to her ear.

"You look incredible." He was tempted to throw her over his shoulder caveman style and carry her to their room. Screw the pictures and the party. But there was still the toast, which was too important to abandon. Once he nailed that, he could focus all his attention on Kate.

The sudden image of Kate naked and in his bed flooded his head and caused all his muscles to stand at attention. He envisioned all the ways he'd finally be able to touch and tease her. He cleared his throat loudly in an attempt to distract his attention before everyone noticed his visible arousal.

"Are you OK?" Kate raised a hand to his cheek. The click of the camera confirmed the photographer had memorialized the moment, and startled them both back to the present.

"Yes." When they reached the end of the aisle he took her in his arms and pressed a kiss to her temple. "Thank you for helping Morgan today."

"You're welcome. I didn't realize until it was too late that your mom had kind of planned it." She wrinkled her brow. "I'm not sure why she planned it, but it seemed to make Morgan feel better, so I figured it was worth it."

His gut clenched. He knew exactly why his mother had

done it. She was all about appearances. It wasn't good enough that he date Kate, she wanted everyone in the Point to believe the relationship was serious. Especially Judy.

His spine stiffened. They weren't serious, they just…were. Right now he wanted to be with Kate and not worry about the future. Was that so much to ask for?

He sucked in a deep, steadying breath and focused on Kate's face.

A soft smile curled the edges of her lips and she leaned forward to kiss him. He wrapped his arms around her and lost himself in the feeling of her soft body against his.

Margaret's voice pierced the air. "Time for pictures."

He dropped his arms from around Kate's waist and turned to see his mother directing a stream of attendants to gather near the white flower archway.

Guests flooded the secluded path to the hotel, where drinks and dancing waited for them.

He turned back to Kate with a smile. Alone. His breath caught. In a few more hours he'd be alone with Kate. Then he'd show her exactly how he felt about her.

CHAPTER EIGHTEEN

Kate was watching Michael and Morgan pose together in front of the crashing waves when an arm snaked around her waist. James's scent hit her, and her body instinctively relaxed into his. She rested her head back against his chest as he wrapped both arms around her waist. His breath was warm on her bare neck, igniting every nerve ending in her body.

"Hi." His voice was husky, intimate.

Her heart skipped a beat. "Hi."

He brushed his lips over her neck, sending tingles down her spine. Then he traced a finger down her bare shoulder and over her arm. She trembled against him.

"Ticklish?"

She fixed her gaze on the ocean and willed herself not to turn and press her body against his. "Wouldn't you like to know?"

He ran another finger down her arm and her legs tremored beneath her. Each featherlight touch brought her closer to dissolving into a pool of longing. When he lowered his mouth to her ear, she had to suppress a moan.

She took a step away and spun to face him, putting a few inches between them. "You'd better keep your hands to yourself. There are people here."

"I can't help it." He spoke in a hoarse whisper. His dark gaze burned into her and she shivered despite the heat on the beach.

She clenched her eyes closed. She needed a second to collect herself, and looking at him, tall and well muscled in his tuxedo, chased all rational thoughts from her head.

There was a crunching of sand and then his slow, steady breathing surrounded her. Desire pooled deep inside her and she opened her eyes.

Even beneath his white tuxedo shirt, she could see the outline of the hard muscles in his chest. His Adam's apple bobbed as he swallowed and took another step toward her.

Her lungs constricted, making it hard to breathe.

She settled her head on his chest below the hollow of his throat. She'd come to think of this as her spot. She fit perfectly and everything felt safe when she was enveloped there.

Behind them someone coughed softly.

She turned in his arms and saw Laurie, who glanced sheepishly to her feet. "Hey, sorry to interrupt, but Margaret said they don't need any more pictures of us. We can go to the reception."

Greg trotted up next to them, a jubilant smile stretched across his face. "We're free! Let's get this party started."

He launched himself into the air and in the direction of

James. Adrenaline flooded her veins and she tried to dodge out of the way, but he hit James from behind and sent him lurching into her. James's strong fingers closed around her wrist as he twisted out of his brother's tackle.

Greg toppled onto the sand, where he lay heaving.

"They're having a moment!" Laurie glowered down at her husband, making no effort to help him up.

"They're always having a moment! It's time for us to have some fun!" Greg bounced back to his feet, grabbed Kate's hand, and started to pull her toward the reception hall.

She ground her heels into the sand.

"Are you OK?" James's eyes were full of concern.

She used her free hand to dust herself off. Her fingers brushed against something ragged. She glanced down. One of the seams had ripped.

Giggles overtook her. "Laurie!"

Laurie's eyes widened in shock before she dissolved into laughter. "Damn it, Greg! Why can't you calm down for thirty seconds? Look what you did!"

Greg frowned as he stared at the torn dress. His cheeks reddened before an impish smile crossed his face. "You're going to be in so much trouble with my mom!"

The threat pushed her into a fresh round of giggles. He'd have to do better than that to scare her.

She shrugged. "I give up. I made it through the wedding and the pictures, and I don't think this dress can take any more torture. I'm going to change." If she tried to wear the bridesmaid dress even five minutes longer, nakedness was inevitable. She was lucky her sewing had lasted this long.

James fixed her with his gray eyes. "Do you need help?"

Mental images from her dreams featuring James flooded her memory and produced an ache low in her belly. Did she want him to help her undress? Yes, please.

"Hell, no." Greg grabbed his brother by the arm. "We have to give a speech and if you two go to your hotel room, I'm not convinced you'll come back out."

Kate's face burned, although she knew he was right. They had only to make it through the rest of the night and then she'd have James to herself.

"Oh my God, it's unraveling here, too." Laurie grabbed at the other side of Kate's dress and pinched two pieces of fabric together. "We better hurry before you're naked."

Her comment sent Kate into another wave of giggles.

"Come on, then, let's go before I flash everybody!" They scurried up the walkway to the hotel.

* * *

James glared at Greg, who dropped his gaze and kicked at the sand.

"I'm sorry I body-slammed your girlfriend."

Girlfriend. The word made his collar itch, but he ignored it. Instead he worked to keep his mouth set in a grim line. "You're lucky she didn't mind."

Greg watched him from the corner of his eye, a small smile on his lips. "Nah, she's tough. And she has a sense of humor."

Warmth filled his chest. It was true. Kate was different from any woman he'd ever met.

The mental image of her standing on the beach while her pink dress unraveled flooded his mind. He allowed himself a grin. Thank God his mom hadn't seen. Although his mom seemed to have developed a soft spot for Kate.

"Let me buy you a drink." Greg draped an arm over his shoulder.

He shrugged out of his brother's sweaty grasp. "It's an open bar."

"Exactly!" Greg sprinted up the path to the hotel.

James chuckled and jogged after him.

They were standing at the bar, waiting in line for their drinks, when he spotted Kate and Laurie across the outdoor tent.

He zeroed in on her immediately. She wore a gold-colored dress with a plunging V in the back and his fingers tingled with the desire to trace the exposed skin. The sight of her in that dress set his nerves on fire.

He watched the way her hips swayed as she walked. His collar grew tight and he had to reach to undo the button. Damn bow tie was going to strangle him.

By the time she reached his side, his body was ablaze.

She bit her lip and reached for his hand. "Hey."

"Hey." Rather than taking her hand, he pulled her into his side and placed his palm on the small of her back. His pulse pounded as his fingertips pressed against her soft, silky skin.

The bartender turned his attention to them. "What can I get you all?"

James ordered for all of them. "Two gin and tonics with lime, one soda water with lime, and a whiskey neat."

"My favorite drink. Are you sure this is a good idea?" She raised an eyebrow at him.

"Absolutely. I've heard you're a super-friendly drunk." He grinned at her.

"Are you saying I'm normally unfriendly, James Abell?" She looked at him, her dark eyes glittering. She parted her lips slightly, as if to say something else, and his body pulsed with anticipation.

At that moment the bandleader tapped on the microphone. "Ladies and gentlemen, I'd ask that you all take your seats, so we can introduce the newlyweds!"

Laurie motioned to them. "We're supposed to line up outside the tent, so the DJ can introduce the wedding party. Margaret's orders."

They hastily gulped their drinks and joined the line of bridesmaids in pink dresses and groomsmen in tuxedos.

Kate nervously tugged at the hem of her dress. "Is your mom going to kill me? I'm the only one who changed."

He circled her waist with one arm. "Don't worry. I'll protect you from her."

The gold dress was a hell of a lot hotter on her anyway.

Couple by couple the DJ made his way down the list of attendants.

"Co–best man Greg Abell and Laurie Abell!"

The crowd applauded politely while they stepped onto the dance floor. When they reached the middle, Greg spun Laurie away from him with a flick of his wrist. They struck a pose, each with one arm outstretched.

So that's how it is. If Greg wanted a competition, he'd give

Greg a competition. His brother was better at a lot of things, but James had always been the better dancer.

"Do you know how to dance?" he whispered to Kate.

Her eyes widened and her eyebrows shot up, but the bandleader drowned out any response. "Co—best man James Abell and Kate Massie!"

He tugged her onto the dance floor. He had this. "Follow my lead."

When they reached the center, he twirled Kate and dipped her.

From her position perpendicular to the floor, Kate stared back at him openmouthed. He left her suspended for a few seconds before he guided her upright, grasped her arm, and led her to a table.

"And I thought I was the competitive one…" She smoothed her hands over her dress and her hair.

He shrugged. "I can't let my brother have all the fun."

She narrowed her eyes and glanced around the room. "I'm now a little afraid of the speeches. Will there be jugglers? Fire breathers? Lions, tigers, and bears? What does it take to win a wedding toast in the Abell family?"

He chuckled. That was why the dance move had been necessary. His brother was infinitely better at public speaking, and James couldn't let him steal all the glory.

They found their seats at the round table with Greg, Laurie, and his parents. A muscle in his jaw ticced and he took a long swig of ice water. No more alcohol until after the toasts. He'd learned that lesson.

A bead of sweat trickled down the back of his neck. He

designed military jets for a living, he'd just flashed some im-
promptu dance moves, and he faced his mother every day.
Why was a simple toast so damn terrifying?

He jiggled his leg under the table, slightly vibrating their
water glasses.

His mother glared at him and Kate placed a hand on his
knee, stilling his leg. "You did write this out?"

He sighed. "Yes, I've been working on it for months. Only
when I'm sober, of course." This wasn't going to be a repeat of
Greg and Laurie's wedding. This time he was prepared.

She squeezed his leg. "Then you have nothing to be nervous
about. You're an expert on Morgan and Michael."

Nervous energy coursed through him and he tapped his fingers on the tabletop, unable to be still.

"How do you do this?" How did she find the energy and the
courage? "Speaking in court, how do you do it?"

Kate frowned and twisted a strand of hair around her finger.
"Certain things need to be said. I only say what's necessary to
make people understand. Then I sit my ass back down before I
ruin it."

The pounding in his temple suddenly stopped.

When Kate put it that way, it sounded easy. Every word he'd
written, everything he'd planned to say, was necessary. Morgan
and Michael needed to hear how much everyone loved them,
how everyone saw the special quality of their relationship.

The bandleader came back on the microphone. "Now an-
nouncing the newlyweds, Morgan and Michael Mooney!"

He swiveled to see Michael leading his sister onto the floor.
The bandleader launched into a Frank Sinatra song and he fo-

cused all his attention on the dancing couple. They stumbled across the floor, Morgan whispering instructions into Michael's ear. The whole Abell family had tried to teach him to dance, but it had proved hopeless.

When the bandleader crooned the final notes, he directed his attention to their table. "At this time I'd like to welcome Greg and James Abell for the best man speeches!"

Greg clapped him on the shoulder. "All right, baby brother, you ready to do this?"

He straightened his bow tie and cracked his knuckles. "I'm always ready to kick your ass."

He grinned at Greg, who shook his head. They walked to the microphone together.

When James turned to face the crowd, his heart beat loudly. *Say what needs to be said, then sit your ass back down.* That couldn't be so hard. He shuffled the white index cards in his hands. He'd made them in advance this time and stored two copies in his suit pockets, in case he lost one.

Greg wrapped his fingers around the microphone and pulled it from the stand. "Most of you know that the Abells have a tendency to marry our high school sweethearts. In fact I think our mom and Judy have been planning this wedding since Morgan and Michael were in middle school."

The crowd laughed. Most of them also knew Greg wasn't entirely kidding. James and Brooke had been subjected to the same crushing pressure.

But not anymore.

"I'd be remiss in my groomsman duties if I failed to mention Morgan and Michael's first high school dance. Mom had ordered us to make an excuse and leave the room immediately if we were alone with them, that way they'd have a chance to ask each other."

Where had Greg learned the word *remiss*? Had he bought a thesaurus just for this toast?

"Unfortunately, Morgan and Michael were both too nervous, and the night before the dance neither of them had a date. So my mom and Judy took matters into their own hands. Judy bought Michael a corsage, put him in a tux, and drove him to our house, where our mom stuffed Morgan in the car next to him. To this day we don't know if they ever asked each other out or if they just bowed to the pressure of the universe and became a couple."

He covered the microphone with one hand and loudly whispered to them. "Wait. This wedding is real, right? You did ask her to marry you, didn't you, Michael?"

Morgan rolled her eyes and smiled at him, while the crowd roared with laughter.

"My point is, you two were meant to be together. It's been obvious to all of us forever. Michael, I'm glad to be the first one to officially welcome you to the family. And Morgan, I'm proud to be your brother. I know you'll keep the family tradition of first loves and happy marriages alive. To you!" He raised his glass and everyone else followed. The dining room echoed with the sound of clinking glasses.

Michael handed the microphone to James. With Kate's words in his head, he stuffed the note cards back into his pocket. He didn't need them. "If you were at my brother's wedding, then you know why Michael needed two best men.

I'm talented when it comes to putting my foot in my mouth."

The crowd guffawed and he relaxed slightly.

He allowed the laughter to die down. "I don't know a lot about marriage, but I do know a lot about Morgan and Michael. When we were little, Morgan and Michael used to love Mr. Rogers. Brooke and I pretended we were too cool for it, but we watched it anyway. After all, we were just being good older siblings." More laughter.

He clenched the microphone harder, trying to mask the shaking of his hands. "There was this song he used to sing called 'It's You I Like.' In honor of Morgan and Michael, I wrote their own version. It goes like this."

He swallowed the lump in his throat, opened his mouth, and began to sing.
It's not the movies that you watch,
It's not the way you drink your Scotch,
It's you I like.
Who you are today
Deep down in your heart—
It's not the video games you play,
It's not the crazy things you say,
It's you I like.
Your thoughts, your heart, your mind,
All the things that make you you,
Today and every day
I like all the parts of you.

He gestured to the bridal party, and they joined him in the refrain, singing, "It's you I like."

Morgan beamed and sobbed at the same time.

"That song will always remind me of the two of you because it perfectly describes the way you love each other. Sometimes I see Michael looking at Morgan when she doesn't notice or I hear the excitement in Morgan's voice when she talks about leaving work and going home to Michael. You don't just love each other, you really like each other. What you have is real. It's the type of love most people dream of. I'm so happy for you both. Let's all raise a glass to Morgan and Michael Mooney and to true love!"

Everyone toasted.

In that moment it hit him.

What they had was what he wanted. And for the first time, it was within his reach.

CHAPTER NINETEEN

Kate tapped her shoe impatiently. The maid of honor stood at the microphone, next to James and Greg, and her speech was cringeworthy. Kate fought the urge to flinch, choosing instead to take a large sip of her fresh gin and tonic.

"...one time, when my boyfriend dumped me, I showed up at Morgan's apartment. Michael was there, watching *The Notebook* with her, and I was just so jealous."

Dear God. It was like a guide on what not to say in a wedding speech. *Short and simple, people. Keep it about the couple.*

Her mind turned to James's speech. He'd been incredible: calm, poised, and charismatic. His words had brought tears to her eyes. And who knew he could sing? After the story from Greg and Laurie's wedding, she'd been genuinely concerned for him.

"Then, another time, I got dumped..."

Kate bit the inside of her cheek. *Don't laugh.* Someone

should snatch the microphone from the bridesmaid and put her out of her misery. Or just turn it off. Kate's gaze darted around the tent. Was there a plug she could pull?

She locked eyes with James and her pulse pounded as she held his gaze. All thoughts of bridesmaid rescue missions fled her head.

Margaret leaned across the table and whispered, "Soon enough it'll be your turn, Kate! I hope you're taking notes."

Her heart lodged in her throat. What? Had Margaret lost her mind?

She swallowed, but it did nothing to relieve the tightness in her chest.

"Drink this." Laurie shoved the gin and tonic into her hand and she gulped it down.

Her face burned and she was careful not to look Margaret directly in the eye. "We haven't talked about that."

The corners of Margaret's mouth dropped. "Still, it never hurts to be prepared." She winked and turned her attention back to the speeches.

Knots of anxiety tangled in her stomach.

Laurie squeezed her hand. "Don't worry about her, she means well."

Kate opened her mouth, then snapped it shut again.

No. Just no. She didn't want to get married. Not now. Maybe not ever. Unlike the Abells, she knew how easy it was for a family to fall apart.

"Congratulations to Michael and Morgan!" The bridesmaid lifted her glass, signaling the official end to her hara-kiri of a wedding toast.

Kate inhaled, held her breath, and exhaled slowly. *Don't worry about Margaret.*

She took another sip of gin and tonic and focused on James. The way his tuxedo jacket hung from his broad shoulders and chest triggered an ache low in her belly.

He gave Morgan and Michael another hug, then covered the distance to their table in a few long strides. He leaned toward her. "I thought that would never end."

She let his familiar scent wash over her and felt the muscles in her neck relax.

"As if anybody could follow the toast you gave and not look bad. Nervous? Are you kidding me? You were incredible!" She squeezed his muscular arm. Goose bumps broke out over her skin.

The tips of his ears reddened as he took a swig of champagne. "Thanks. I worked hard on it."

She leaned forward to whisper in his ear. "You almost made me cry."

He reared back, his eyes wide. "Kate Massie crying? I don't believe it."

She grabbed his arm and pulled him to her, dropping the volume of her voice. "Shh, don't tell anyone. You'll ruin my reputation, and I've worked very hard to build my street cred. Plus I said *almost* cried. You'll have to work harder than that to make me cry."

James's gray eyes softened and he raised a hand to cup her cheek. "What if I promise never to make you cry?"

The back of her throat burned and she looked away, focusing her attention on the ground. Why did people make promises that were impossible to keep?

She gave a quick nod and he kissed her gently on the lips before he dropped his hand.

A server appeared with plates of salad, which he placed in front of them.

"Kate, do you know how long our family has been in Belmont?" Kent threw back his snifter of whiskey and followed it with the rest of his champagne.

She glanced at James, who kept his eyes carefully fixed on his plate. Was this a trick question? Or Belmont trivia time?

Out of the corner of her eye she caught a flash of movement. Greg formed the numbers one, zero, and five with his fingers.

"A hundred years?"

"Exactly! One hundred and five years of Abells in Belmont. We founded Abell and Davidson and now that rat bastard wants to force me out of my family's own business."

Davidson. A chill went down her spine. That was Nico's last name.

The waiter appeared with a bottle of wine and Margaret gave Kent's empty glass a pointed look, then waved the server away.

Kate forced aside the uneasy feeling. Davidson was a common last name. There were probably lots of Davidsons in Belmont.

She glanced around the table. What was she supposed to say now?

"You're going to start your own Abell family business, Dad. Besides, we can't talk business at your only daughter's wedding. You and Mom should tell us more about the vacation you're planning." Under the table James threaded his fingers with hers.

She let out a long breath and leaned into his shoulder. Only a few more hours.

* * *

James wrapped an arm around Kate, relishing the feel of her warm body contoured against his. His family had made it through the full wedding dinner without any fights or major awkwardness. The home stretch was in sight.

Onstage the guitarist struck the first chord and the bandleader crooned into the microphone.

Kate jumped to her feet and grabbed his hand, her eyes sparkling with excitement. "Let's dance!"

With a grin he allowed her to lead him onto the dance floor. Greg and Laurie followed, Greg with his drink clasped firmly in his hand. James shook his head to himself. In an hour most of his family would be drunk. Another Abell family wedding tradition.

He joined Kate as she swayed and twisted to the music. Her arms stayed one step ahead of her feet, and she had a wide array of strange dance moves, including one that resembled the action of a sprinkler. Despite her lack of coordination, she grinned and danced enthusiastically. When the bandleader launched into "Do the Funky Chicken," she even flapped her arms.

All the anxiety he'd carried over the last week melted from

his body as he danced with her. He was mesmerized by her carefree easiness.

As she swayed from side to side, she raised a hand and made a wavelike motion. Without thinking, he raised his own hand and imitated her.

She caught his eye and grinned. "It's called the showboat. Beth and I invented it in seventh grade."

She did a little shimmy from side to side and a dip. "That one is the Kate."

He wiggled his hips from side to side, then imitated the dip.

Laurie and Greg crowded next to them, creating a small circle.

"What are we doing?" Laurie asked.

Kate smirked. "Oh, I'm just teaching James how to dance."

"I want to play!" Laurie clapped her hands like a small child.

Kate motioned her to the center of their little group. "Go ahead, make up a move and teach it to the rest of us."

Laurie paused for a second, biting her lip. Then she threw her hands in the air and swiveled her hips. "I call this the tootsie roll!"

Soon they were all inventing ridiculous dance moves and teaching them to one another. Several songs later they were all sweaty and red-faced.

He wiggled his feet in his dress shoes. They'd begun to pinch, and his toes felt as if they might fall off.

He slid one arm around Kate's waist and pressed his mouth close to her ear, inhaling the orange scent of her shampoo. "Do you want another drink? I need to take a break for a second."

She hooked her arm through his. "A break sounds excellent.

I need some ice water." She fanned herself with her free hand. "Being this fantastic at dancing is hard work."

He met her eye and they both broke into laughter. Who cared if she was a good dancer?

They joined the line at the bar and he wrapped his arms around her, pulling her into his chest. Rather than snuggling into her normal spot at the hollow of his neck, she held his gaze. Her lips parted and his pulse pounded as she pressed her mouth to his. He cupped her face in his hands and tilted her chin toward him, pushing his tongue deeper. Their tongues tangled together and his hands trailed to her hips, urging her body forward.

Blood rushed below his waist and he had to rip himself away from her before he went too far. He jammed his hands into his pockets and rocked on the balls of his feet. God, he wished they were alone.

Kate's face fell and she diverted her gaze, focusing on the dance floor.

Damn it. He gritted his teeth and searched the crowd for Michael and Morgan.

What time was it? How long until they could slip away undetected?

He ordered their drinks, then led the way to their table. Greg was slumped forward. Laurie held a glass of water in one hand and tried to prop his head up with the other.

James plopped into the chair next to her. "You need some help?"

She shoved the glass into his hand. "Have at it. Maybe you'll have better luck than me."

He studied his brother's messy hair. Had he already crossed the line from fun drunk to sloppy drunk?

He put his hand under his brother's chin and forced it up. "Drink this." He shoved the water under Greg's face.

Greg lowered his mouth and slurped from it, like an animal from a trough.

He bit back a laugh. New plan. Was it time to carry Greg to bed? At least then he and Kate would have an excuse to get out of here.

With laser focus Greg looked to Kate. "You wanna play Beirut?"

She gestured to the crowded dance floor. "Sorry, Greg, I'm a little busy now. In a minute James and I are going to dance some more."

"Oh yeah, let's dance!" He grabbed the water glass, stood, and charged into the middle of the dancing crowd.

"Shit." Laurie popped up and ran after him.

A shattering sound rang through the air and people stopped dancing to flee in all directions, leaving Greg and a large puddle of water. Shards of glass littered the floor around him.

Laurie froze a few feet away, her face bright red.

Then Greg gave a shrug and wandered over to her. "I guess nobody's dancing anymore."

Next to him Kate snorted and clapped a hand over her mouth. Her shoulders shook with suppressed laughter.

With a smirk James leaned closer to her. "That is what we, in the Abell family, call inevitable."

Laurie gripped Greg by the elbow and propelled him to their table. "Say good night to James and Kate."

Greg pouted. "Do I have to?"

He stood and grabbed his brother's other arm. Laurie would need help getting Greg to their room. "Afraid so, big guy."

Laurie waved him off. "I have him. And if I don't, I'll pay a bellboy to shove him on the luggage cart and wheel him up to the room. You all stay and have fun."

He hesitated. This was part of his Abell family job description.

Then he glanced at Kate. His eyes traced the scoop of her gold dress, the hint of cleavage peeking from the neckline, the curve of her hips. Adrenaline coursed through him. Decision made. He was done cleaning up after his family for the night.

He folded Kate's hand in his and gently tugged her to her feet. "Come with me."

He led her out of the tent and into the cool night air. When they reached the path to the beach he paused so she could slip her feet from her shoes. Her hair shimmered in the moonlight and the sound of crashing waves filled the air.

They made their way down to the beach. Stars dotted the sky and the sand crunched beneath his shoes.

He faced her, wrapped one arm around her waist, and positioned her right hand so it rested on his shoulder. He took her other and closed his large fingers around her thin, slender ones. For a long moment he stared into her eyes while his pulse thundered in his ears.

He swallowed hard as she settled her head against his chest. With the fingers of her right hand she traced the muscles of his shoulder, stoking the fire inside him.

He placed his right hand on the small of her back, savoring the warmth of her skin under his fingers.

"You have to hold on tight and follow my lead." He took a step to the right. After a second she followed.

He counted in his head as he swept her across the sand in a formal ballroom box step. Her body relaxed in his arms.

"I'm going to twirl you now," he whispered into her hair. He released her left hand and lifted his arm so he could guide her through the spin. When she turned back, she had a grin on her face.

His heart thudded in his chest. She was gorgeous, all sparkly and glowing in the light of the stars and the moon.

"And this is where I dip you." He secured an arm around her waist and slowly tipped her backward. Her body was languid in his arms as she closed her eyes and gave herself over to his touch.

He held her there for a long moment, drinking in the swell of her breasts and the contours of her waist and hips.

When he lifted her again, she wrapped her arms around his neck and clung to him.

"Where did you learn to dance?"

Every inch of him was aware of her body pressed against his as they swayed softly to the music. "My mom insisted Greg and I take ballroom dance lessons when we were in middle school."

She giggled. "Greg took them, too? You can't tell."

He tried to slow his breathing, which was ragged to his own ears. "Yeah, he was awful. I think it was the only thing I was better at as a kid."

"I seriously doubt that." Her voice was soft.

The song stopped and the band launched into something faster, but the two of them continued to hold each other, swaying from side to side. He lifted a hand and ran it over her silky hair.

This was his chance. For the first time in two weeks there was no family, no well-meaning friends, no made-up relationships, no exes, no misguided sense of obligation. It was just him and Kate.

The possibilities felt endless.

CHAPTER TWENTY

Her body tingled as she pressed harder against him and his tongue slid into her mouth. She slipped her arms inside his tuxedo jacket and wound them around his waist, then pressed her breasts against his chest and tilted her chin to deepen the kiss. Stars exploded behind her eyes.

His hands stroked her hips, and her breath hitched. Her body pulsed with desire as she rocked into his hardness.

She nipped at his lips, and his fingers dug into her waist, urging her closer. He let his other hand wander, exploring her neck, her shoulders, her arms, then down to her waist. Her senses flooded with awareness of him: his scent, his taste, the feel of his body pressed against hers.

He lowered his head into her hair and breathed raggedly next to her ear. "Please, let's get out of here."

She turned into him, so her lips hovered over the bare skin of his neck. "Do we need to say good-bye to anyone?"

His mouth skimmed along her jawline, sending her heart

racing. "Hell no. They'll all still be here in the morning."

A shiver ran down her spine. "Then what are you waiting for?"

They ran through the sand, hand in hand, to the hotel's side entrance, avoiding the crowd under the tent.

James dug through his pants pocket. "Shit." He shoved a hand in the other pocket and flipped it inside out.

"Let me look." Kate stepped toward him and undid the buttons on his jacket. She ran her hands over his chest, her mouth watering over the hard planes.

His breath caught as she stepped forward and dipped her fingers into the interior suit pocket.

Her finger brushed something smooth and plastic.

Shit. She'd been hoping it would require a little more searching.

She stepped back and held it out to him, pinched between two fingers. "I found it, but I can keep looking."

His pupils dilated.

After a long moment he plucked the card from her hands and jammed it into the key reader. "I have better plans for us."

He held the door for her and the minute she stepped inside, his hands were all over her. He kissed her fiercely, pushing forward until her head bumped against the wall behind her.

He tore his mouth from hers. "Are you OK?"

In answer she pressed her lips against his and plunged her tongue into his mouth. This wasn't a time for talking. Every atom in her body screamed with the need to taste more, feel more.

He ran his hands over her hips to cup her butt, then back

up again so he could trace his thumbs over the fabric covering her breasts. His mouth traveled across her neck and his tongue was powerful as it caressed her skin. He followed the V of the dress's neck, covering every inch of exposed skin.

Her body was tense and needy as she arched against him. Pure desire thrummed through her veins as she closed her eyes and lost herself to sensation.

"That feels even better than I remembered." Her voice was a murmur.

He stopped, her skin suddenly cold where his mouth had been.

Shit. She'd said that out loud, hadn't she?

She forced her eyes open, only to find him staring at her, longing written in every detail of his expression.

She gave a slow smile. "From my dreams." She captured his mouth with hers, while she ripped his shirttails from his pants and shoved her hands inside the fabric. She gasped at the solid ridges of his abdomen and the trail of hair leading from his chest, down his belly, to…She growled with frustration. She needed him out of his pants. Now.

He caught her face in his hands and smirked at her. "You had a dream about me." His voice was a low growl. A statement, not a question.

She licked her lips and nodded.

"When?"

They stared at one another. His dark hair was mussed and she longed to run her fingers through it.

Instead she trailed a finger over his jawline, watching as the muscles worked.

"After I saw you at the gym." She swallowed. "Before the time I saw you with Ainsley."

He caught her hands in his and held them, stilling her fingers. His eyes burned with intensity. "Good. Because I saw you, too."

Any remaining restraint she possessed fractured, unleashing a flood of desire.

His hungry mouth crashed into hers and his tongue teased her past the threshold of rationality. Her legs liquefied, and it was all she could do to stand. She clung to his shoulders, clenched the strong muscles of his upper arms, in an effort to stay upright.

She jerked her mouth from his. "Take me to the room."

Normally the vulnerability in her voice would have terrified her, but right now she didn't give a damn.

He flashed a grin before the hungry look returned to his eyes. "You know, I remember exactly the way you looked the first time I met you all those years ago. I remember you smelled like strawberries and your hair fell in wisps around your face. And I remember you wore this black dress and had the most incredible legs." He placed a hand on her thigh and slid it up her leg.

Her breath hitched and her mind whirled. "You remember what I was wearing?"

His hand strayed farther upward and when he reached the spot where the waistband of her underwear would have been, he groaned. "God, yes. You were gorgeous. You are gorgeous."

She melted into his touch. One small thrust and his fingers would be exactly where she needed them. "So take me upstairs." Her voice was almost a gasp. She couldn't wait any longer. "Please."

His eyelids went heavy and she could feel his heart pounding in his chest.

Without a word he grabbed her hand and pulled her up the stairs behind him.

When they reached the door to the room, he already had the key card in hand. He jammed it into the reader and yanked it back out, all in one swift motion. He smiled as he held the door for her, his eyes raking over her body. The force of his gaze sent a delicious shiver through her.

Before the door clicked shut behind them, his mouth was on hers and her hands were ripping at his clothing.

She fumbled with the shirt buttons, which slipped through her fingers. She pulled her mouth away from his and focused her attention on the buttons, her fingers working to slide them from their holes. He watched her, his chest heaving up and down as the air crackled between them.

Kate moved slowly, purposefully torturing him. When his bare chest came into view, she pressed her mouth against it and let her tongue taste his exposed skin. He tasted salty, like sweat, but sweet at the same time.

She ran her hands, palms open, over his torso.

He dropped his head back and let out a groan. His eyes were closed and the muscles around his mouth twitched when her palms found an area previously unexplored.

Her hands moved to his pants and his eyes snapped open. He watched her greedily as she popped the button and unzipped his fly. He shrugged out of them in one swift move.

The look in his eyes sent another flash of heat through her body. Suddenly her dress was like a straightjacket. She needed to feel him, skin against skin.

She placed her hand inside his pants and brushed her fingers against his hardness. He tensed for a second, then tilted his hips and guided his penis fully into her grasp. Liquid heat pooled between her legs.

He was rock-hard in her hand and she trembled against him. Desire spread like hot water inside her, seeping into every nook, until it possessed her completely.

She tightened her fingers around his penis and stroked slowly, once, then twice. He shuddered and grabbed her, pulling her body into his. "Not yet."

He wrapped his arms around her and reached to unzip her dress. As he inched it down, he traced the contours of her body with his hands.

The dress fell into a puddle around her feet and his eyes raked over her, sending another wave of heat through her body. She should have felt exposed, vulnerable. Instead she felt powerful. James looked at her exactly as she'd always hoped a man would: as if she were the most beautiful woman alive.

She stepped toward him, leaving the dress behind her. His eyes were dark, his expression serious. With one hand he cupped her neck and with the other he supported the small of her back as he lowered her onto the bed.

He knelt over her and unhooked the front clasp of her strapless bra. Her breasts spilled into his waiting hands, aching for his touch. His thumbs teased her nipples as his mouth lowered to meet them and flicked across their surfaces. The sensation surged to her core. Kate arched her back, encouraging him to take more of her in his mouth. Heat and need and want coursed through her. Her body had become a separate entity, almost entirely outside her control.

Her skin sang as James touched her, his fingers leaving trails of fire in their wake. Pleasure lapped at her toes, building in intensity and flooding her body. Kate ached to be surrounded by him, every part of her body subsumed into James. Without thinking, she thrust her hips upward, begging him to enter her.

* * *

James drank in Kate's face: her eyes hazy with desire, her cheeks flushed, and her lips swollen from kissing. She closed her eyes and arched her neck, sending adrenaline crashing through his body.

He grabbed a condom out of the nightstand and unrolled it over the length of his penis. Her eyes flickered open and she watched him, her lips parting as she studied his movements.

Her eyes bored into him. "Please, James."

The low hum of her voice electrified him. He planted his forearms on either side of her shoulders and buried his head in her neck as he rocked into her.

She gasped and lifted her hips off the bed, pushing him deeper. The movement ignited everything inside him and he had to force himself to stroke slowly, into her and then away from her.

He ran his hands over her nipples and her rib cage, nipping

at the soft skin of her shoulders, eager to experience every inch of her. Kate became soft and pliant, yielding under his touch.

With one hand she gripped his hip, angling him into her, while she kept the other wrapped around his neck, focusing his gaze on her eyes. As if he could have looked anywhere else.

Each time he rocked away she grabbed his hip harder, her fingers digging into his skin, as she thrust up to meet him. Steadily she increased the pace of their movements.

She let her eyelids flicker closed. "I love"—her voice caught—"the way you smell."

Her words pierced him and his throat grew thick.

For a long moment he caressed the smooth skin of her face, drinking in her features. "I love the way you smell."

With a small smile she opened her eyes and ran her hands over the hard planes of his chest, the thick muscles in his arms, and down his hips to grasp his butt. She followed the path of her hands with her eyes and when she thrust into him, pushing him even deeper than before, his control cracked. He lost himself, giving in to his body's natural rhythm. Kate clung to him, her fingernails piercing the skin of his back. It was a heady combination of pleasure and pain.

He bit back the peak of his desire and forced himself to slow. He refused to come alone. He lowered his hand between her legs and used his thumb to stroke her clitoris. The nub was slick and swollen under his touch. Kate moaned as spasms rolled through her body. She clutched him wildly, her fingernails scraping over his skin. The muscles inside her cradled his hardness, gently stroking him toward the point of climax.

She broke first, her plaintive cries echoing through the

room. He buried his head in the skin of her neck and let the ecstasy overtake him as he joined her, his body exploding into a thousand pieces.

"Kate. Holy shit, Kate." He heard himself growling her name over and over, as if the sound came from somewhere outside him.

When his body stopped shuddering, he rolled onto his back and pulled her against his chest.

She nuzzled against him, one hand tracing the bare skin of his torso.

"Holy shit," she panted. "That was amazing."

A warm wave of satisfaction rolled over him.

He stroked her hair. "You're amazing."

Her body against him consumed every piece of his awareness. He traced the freckles on her shoulder, then followed the curve of her stomach and her hip. "You are so beautiful."

She was so much more than that, but the right words evaded his grasp. Why couldn't he find them?

Kate pulled her hair over her face, like a curtain. Too bad. She'd have to get used to receiving compliments.

He brushed her hair back so he could see her. "You are. You're so beautiful."

She blushed but met his gaze. She took a deep breath and let it out slowly. "You're amazing."

Then she glanced away and bit her lip.

He had to fight against the triumphant laugh that threatened to burst out of him.

"You make me happy." She ran her fingers over his chest and began to draw small patterns on his skin. "You make me crazy happy. You're sexy and kind and funny and thoughtful and oh, I don't know."

His lungs squeezed painfully. So why was she so nervous?

He grabbed her hand and lifted it to his mouth. She could trust him. He wouldn't hurt her.

"Does that make you nervous?"

"God, yes. It makes me terrified." She lowered her lashes.

He put a finger under her chin and tilted her face up to meet his gaze. "I'm not going to hurt you."

Tears gathered in the corners of her eyes and she refused to meet his gaze.

"OK." She nuzzled back into his chest.

Whatever it took, he would prove it to her.

CHAPTER TWENTY-ONE

As she floated into wakefulness, Kate became aware of the warm breath on her neck, the muscular body twined with hers, and the hardness jutting into her stomach. Her nipples hardened into peaks and fresh desire pooled between her legs.

She cracked her eyes open. It was still dark out, with only the softest wisps of orange light beginning to filter through. The rays were just enough to illuminate the bulge of his biceps pressed against her and the lines of his six-pack.

Good. That meant she had plenty of time.

She brushed her pebbled nipples against him. No hands and no mouth. She'd use the rest of her body to tease him awake.

She lifted one leg and wrapped it around him, rocking her pelvis into his hardness.

His eyes popped open. His pupils were dilated, and a smile spread across his mouth as his eyes zeroed in on her.

Without a word he wrapped a hand around her butt, supporting the leg that straddled him. He rolled onto his back, pulling her with him, and lifted up to kiss her on the mouth. His tongue teased her lips open and stroked inside her.

She reached for the nightstand, where she'd seen the package of condoms, using the opportunity to press her breasts against his chest.

He let out a low moan. His hands flew to her butt and squeezed.

She tore open the packaging with her teeth and leaned back. This time she'd put it on.

His hard penis bobbed against her belly and she stopped to admire its rigid length. She grasped it firmly in one hand and he writhed underneath her, bucking up and into her body.

Need burst inside her and she quickly rolled the condom onto his penis, then lowered herself onto him.

He groaned and his hands slid down to her hips, pulling him deeper.

Then he lifted one hand to the nape of her neck and crushed her mouth to his.

She rocked against him, acquiescing to the rhythm her body demanded. Last night had been slow and sweet, something to savor. This morning she was possessed by a carnal need. There would be more time for slow and sweet later.

She pinned his shoulders with the palms of her hands and swiveled her hips, taking what she needed.

From the twitch of his muscles and the hazy look in his eyes, she could tell he was getting close. She braced her hands on his chest and leaned back, guiding him to the right spot.

Stars exploded behind her eyes and her muscles spasmed.

She lost control of the rhythm, collapsing into his chest and letting him take control.

He tangled his hands in her hair and took her mouth with his as he lifted his hips up and off the bed. He called her name, long and low, as he pumped into her.

When he finished he gathered her in his arms and cocooned her against his chest. He pressed a kiss to the top of her head.

"You have a magic penis." It was the first thought that popped into her head. *Idiot.*

He chuckled. "Go back to sleep, Katie. It's early and I have big plans for you today."

Go back to sleep? Impossible. She was wide-awake now.

She feathered kisses along his chest. "Let's go for a walk. See the sunrise. Before everyone else is awake."

"I thought you hated mornings?" His voice carried a low note of amusement.

She nuzzled into him. "I do. But I'm awake and I anticipate a nice long nap for both of us later."

He bolted upright, pulling her with him. "Walk on the beach now and nap later? Yes. Maybe two naps."

She giggled as she threw back the covers and lowered her feet to the ground. She reached into her suitcase for a pair of shorts and a T-shirt, which she pulled on. She tied her hair back without brushing it, then raised an eyebrow at him.

"You ready?"

He'd also donned shorts and a T-shirt. "Ready."

He held his hand out to her and she took it, weaving her fingers with his.

She frowned and glanced around the room. Had she left her clutch at the reception hall last night?

Her spine prickled. She had. Well, that was stupid. Although definitely worth it, all things considered.

"Can we swing by the tent? I left my purse and I want to see if it's still there."

He nodded. "Yeah, sure. I think I left my phone on my chair, too."

Thank God this was Belmont, with a nearly 0 percent crime rate. Their things would probably still be there.

They made their way through the halls and down to the reception tent. It was chaos. Tablecloths askew, flower arrangements upended, and trash littering the dance floor.

Her eyes widened. "You all do know how to party."

In the center of the dance floor, one disheveled couple swayed to the tinny music pumping from a cell phone.

His mouth twisted. "My family does, yeah. This kind of chaos isn't necessarily my idea of a good time."

"Oh yeah? What is your idea of a good time?"

His eyes were focused on their table at the other end of the tent. "I just think a wedding should be intimate. About the couple, celebrating with their closest friends and family. Not a magazine spread."

Her stomach twisted as she recalled Margaret's words from the night before. *I hope you're taking notes.*

She swallowed hard. *Don't think about it.* He wasn't talking about his wedding; he was talking about weddings in general. Who even knew if James Abell wanted to get married?

"Aha!" He reached the table first. In one hand he held her sparkly clutch and in the other his phone.

He punched a button on the phone and his eyes narrowed. "Battery died. That figures. Good news is, my mom won't be able to find us."

He wiggled an eyebrow in her direction and shoved the cell phone into his back pocket.

She took the clutch from his hand and dug through it. ID. Twenty dollars cash. And her phone. Exactly as it should be.

She lifted her phone and pushed a button. The screen lit up, showing seven new text messages.

Probably from Beth, wanting details of the night before. She'd give her the dirty details later. She dropped the phone back into her purse and hooked her arm through James's.

"So where should we go?"

He shrugged. "Wherever we want."

They followed the hotel path down to the beach, where they kicked off their flip-flops and left them by the sand shower. They'd get them on the way back.

They walked down the beach in companionable silence. Kate leaned her head against James's arm and lost herself in the pleasure of being near him.

As they walked the sky filled with brighter colors. Pinks and blues and yellows joined the original orange haze. She looked out over the water and saw the bloom of color rising beyond the ocean.

"We should take a picture."

The wind whipped her ponytail into his face and he laughed, pushing her hair aside. "Sunrise selfie?"

"Exactly." She skipped toward the water, letting the cold morning waves lap at her ankles.

She handed him her phone. "Your arms are longer, so you do it."

He took the phone in one hand and wrapped his other arm around her waist. The moment before he pressed the button, he turned to kiss her cheek, making her laugh and squeal.

She swatted his shoulder. "We need one of our faces!"

He gave her a slow lazy grin and brushed his lips against hers. From the phone she heard another click.

"James!" She planted her hands on her hips. Not that she minded the other pictures, but she had a specific one in mind and soon the sun would be up.

"OK, OK." He wrapped his arm around her waist and held the phone out in front of them. She smiled and waited.

Click.

He pulled the phone in and spun it around so she could see the screen. There they were. Both of them wearing big goofy smiles, their eyes sparkling.

Her vision blurred. They looked completely natural together. They looked happy.

Her lungs constricted. How long could that last?

She turned and ran farther into the surf, the chilly water splashing against her shins.

"You're nuts. I'm staying right here and texting myself a copy of the picture," his voice boomed after her.

She kicked at the waves for a few seconds, until her toes grew numb. Then she turned to run back to him.

She froze, her heart climbing into her chest. He stared at

her, the corners of his mouth turned down, his eyes blazing.

She walked to him, her pulse pounding in her ears. What was it? What had changed in thirty seconds?

With every step she steeled herself. When she reached him, the words came flying from her mouth: "What's wrong?"

She clenched her eyes shut. Her voice was small and high-pitched.

He held the phone out to her. "Why didn't you tell me you knew Nico Davidson?"

Her breath grew tight in her chest. Nico? This was about Nico? What had he done now?

She blinked at him. Then his father's words came rushing back to her. The Davidsons were trying to force him out of his business. In everything that followed, she'd completely forgotten.

She bit her lip. Of course it would be weird for James, but she could explain.

"I dated him. Before I moved back here."

His eyes rounded and he took an abrupt step backward. "You dated him?"

She clasped her hands in front of her, willing herself to stay rooted to the spot. She wouldn't chase him and beg him.

"I did. Not for long. We don't really see each other or talk anymore."

Her spine prickled. Had he been going through her phone? What exactly had he seen?

She kept her voice level. "What did you see?"

His eyebrows knitted together. "I saw his name in your text messages. Why, what was there to see?"

The sharpness in his voice sliced through her. This time she took a step back, into the reach of the chilly surf.

She snatched the phone from his hand, pulled the screen up, and thumbed through it. When she found what she wanted, she held it out to him. "Here. Where I tell him I'm seeing someone. And here where he texts me that he knows it's you. You'll notice I didn't respond."

Let him look through her phone. She didn't have anything to hide.

He didn't take it, instead he shook his head and ran a hand through his unruly hair. "You don't have to show me anything. You don't have to prove anything to me. I trust you."

His shoulders slumped and her throat grew dry. He trusted her? It sure didn't feel that way.

Her eyes narrowed. "Why wouldn't you trust me?"

Her words hung in the air, stretching the silence between them.

His forehead creased. "Because the guy is a raging asshole. His family has been in business with our family for generations. But suddenly, now that he's about to finish business school, his dad is staging a coup for the board. They're going to force my dad out after he's spent his entire life working for that business."

Her limbs locked. She'd gathered that much from what Kent and Michael had told her. But what did that have to do with her?

He lowered his gaze and kicked at the sand with his bare feet. "You could have told me you'd dated him."

Her heart skittered. She could have. Maybe she should have.

Belmont was a small town and she'd been naïve to think she could ignore Nico forever. Of course his family knew James's.

So why hadn't she? Her pulse quickened. She should have told him last night, when she'd understood the connection. But that would have meant this was real. When had it become real?

Shit.

The weight of the truth crashed down on her shoulders. This wasn't how things were supposed to be. She struggled to suck in air. That moment when she'd turned from the waves and seen the coldness in his eyes? That was why she couldn't do this. This time it had just been a misunderstanding, but what about the next time? One day he could turn and walk away. Then it wouldn't be thirty seconds of panic and numbness. It would stretch on and on, the pain crushing her.

She pulled the phone back and stuffed it in her pocket.

"Look, Kate." James reached for her, but she sidestepped him. This was a mistake. She had to get out of here and away from him. He clouded her judgment, made her act on instinct and emotion rather than common sense.

"I have to go." Without another look at him, she turned and fled up the beach, running as fast as her legs would take her.

* * *

James stared after her, his mouth hanging open as her figure grew smaller and smaller in the distance.

What the hell? What had just happened here?

He squared his shoulders and clenched his jaw. He would not run after her. This was nuts.

Slowly and deliberately he strode in the direction of the hotel, his mind a storm of conflicting thoughts.

Who was Kate Massie? He thought he knew her. Over the last two weeks he'd seen her happy and sad, strong and weak, hurt and determined. But the wild panic on her face when he'd said he trusted her? That didn't make sense at all.

He looked out at the water. All of a sudden his chest was tight and it felt as if he were drowning, as if someone were holding him under the surf.

He shook his head, chasing the sensation away.

Maybe she'd just done him a favor. He didn't want to be in a relationship with anybody. He'd been swept away by the alcohol and the stress, the hormones and the way she'd looked in that gold dress.

His pulse raced as he remembered her in his bed, the way she'd looked up at him with dark eyes, her breasts heaving.

No. He clenched his hands into fists. He would not torture himself. She was the one who'd run. She was the one who'd freaked out. He was tired of bending over backward and turning his life upside down to make other people happy. After nine years with Brooke, he knew that didn't work.

His throat constricted. Kate wasn't like Brooke. Or was she? Did she want him to chase after her, to beg and plead for a chance to make things right? Did she expect him to jump through hoops that existed only in her mind, until he'd somehow proved himself? He wouldn't do that. Not for her and not for anybody else.

CHAPTER TWENTY-TWO

Kate slammed the door of the taxi closed and dragged her suitcase up the stairs. Wally's bark thundered from inside the house.

When she reached the door and pulled it open, Beth stood inside. She had her messenger bag slung over one shoulder and a cup of coffee in her hand.

Her eyes narrowed when she saw Kate. "It's six a.m., what the hell are you doing awake and why are you back at this house? Don't you have a hotel room with Mr. Sexy?"

The tears spilled over and began to run down her cheeks. She hiccupped as she tried to gain control.

So much for never crying.

Beth rushed to her and wrapped her arms around her. She was so short that her head hit Kate smack in the boobs. Normally they laughed about it, but right now she couldn't muster the tiniest flicker of humor.

"I'm sorry! I have no idea what I said, but I'm sorry!"

Kate sniffled and pressed the heels of her hands into her eyes. Clearly she needed to sleep. This was nuts.

"I'm officially delaying my muffin delivery and sitting here until you tell me what's wrong. If the good people of Belmont don't get their muffins today, I'm going to blame you and your refusal to acknowledge that you have emotions."

Kate wrinkled her nose at her best friend. Typical Beth. She knew how to get right to the point. Her muffin side business was just taking off and Kate wouldn't do anything to jeopardize it.

She flopped backward onto the sofa and Beth perched beside her.

"I'm an idiot. I like to torture myself apparently. I slept with him."

Beth's eyes lit, but she kept her head tilted toward Kate and her lips pressed together.

"It was—" Her throat tightened and her eyes burned. "It was incredible. Perfect. The best sex of my entire life."

The tears spilled over again and this time she didn't try to stop them.

Beth put a hand on her knee and squeezed.

"And then he saw Nico's name in my phone and he was…I don't know. Mad? Disappointed? His dad and Nico's dad own a business together and Nico's dad is trying to force him out. You should have seen the way his face crumpled when I told him I'd dated Nico."

Her stomach wrenched. She didn't know if she'd ever forget that look.

Beth tilted her head to the side. "He was mad? Like really

angry at you?" There was a note of disbelief in her voice.

Kate shook her head. "Only for a second, but it felt longer than that. I showed him my phone and told him what happened with Nico, but he wouldn't look at it. He said he trusted me."

The tears came harder and she dropped her face into her hands.

"You're crying because he said he trusted you?"

She lifted her head. Beth's forehead was furrowed.

She swiped at her eyes. "No, not because he trusted me. I don't know. Because it just felt like I'd disappointed him. And I didn't do anything, at least not on purpose. And the way it felt to disappoint him was…awful. Really awful."

The thought sucked the air from her lungs all over again.

Beth pressed her index finger to her lips for a long second. "So you left? Like broke-up-with-him left?"

She nodded as the burning in her throat intensified.

Here she was, like a lost teenager all over again. When would she finally toughen up?

"Do you think he loves you?" Beth's voice dropped to a whisper.

A sharp, jagged feeling shot through her ribs. It was out of the question. They barely knew each other, of course he didn't love her.

She forced a shrug. "What does it matter? He doesn't trust me."

Beth threw her hands in the air and rolled her eyes. "Now you're just inventing reasons to break up with him."

Kate fixed her with a glare. Why would she do that? She wanted to be with him…didn't she?

Beth smiled knowingly. "You remember when you broke up with Nico?"

Of course she remembered. He'd been nagging her to have dinner with his family, in Belmont, and she'd realized she didn't want to be serious with him. At least not meet-the-parents serious. All of a sudden she'd realized what a waste of time the whole thing was.

She nodded.

Beth gripped her shoulder and looked her directly in the eye. "You broke up with him the second things started to get real. Before he could tell you he loved you. He did love you, I think, from that time I visited. He sort of looked at you like he did. But you broke up with him before you could really care about him."

She snorted. Nico hadn't loved her. Their relationship hadn't been like that. Beth was being overly romantic again.

"He told me he loved you."

She started, nearly jumping from her seat. He'd what? "Why didn't you tell me that?"

Beth sighed. "Because I know you. You haven't gotten close to very many people since your dad died. Think about it. You have me and Rachel. And Ryan, but Ryan's kind of a safe person to love because he's a jackass, but he's a sweet jackass and at least if he hurts you you know it's always accidental. Plus he brings you gluten-free maple bacon doughnuts."

She shrugged. She already knew that. And she also knew she needed to toughen up again, work on her defenses. With James she'd let herself get too soft.

Beth lifted a finger and tapped it against Kate's temple.

"Think about it. You're here on the sofa, with me, crying because you love him and you think he might love you. And instead of going for it and being happy with him, you're going to rip yourself apart trying to shut it down before he can hurt you."

All the muscles in her body tensed.

"Don't you think you're hurting yourself right now more than he could hurt you? And isn't the chance that he might not hurt you worth it?"

Her vision blurred again and hot tears spilled over.

Damn it. Would she ever stop crying? Or were twelve years' worth of tears determined to pour out of her?

Beth squeezed her hand. "Besides, think how good you felt yesterday. That moment of shittiness you felt when he saw Nico's name? Doesn't all of the good from yesterday outweigh that tenfold?"

Emotion clogged her throat and she let out a tiny wail. Beth was right. She'd fucked up.

"Why didn't you tell me?" she managed to choke out.

She turned the words over in her head. *Tell me? Tell me what?* That it was OK to fall in love with someone? That needing somebody wasn't a bad thing? That not everyone would hurt her? All of a sudden the truth was so clear. Being with James was worth it. Whatever happened happened. She was strong, tough. She could handle it.

Beth gave her a small smile. "I thought I just did."

* * *

His legs ached, but he refused to stop. He kept pounding the pavement, forcing himself to some unknown destination.

Actually, he knew the destination. He'd run until he was too tired to think. About Kate, about his life, about any of it. He'd been stewing over their conversation all morning and he wanted his brain to shut up.

His phone dinged in his pocket. He pushed himself harder, pumping his legs faster. No doubt it was his mother, wanting another favor. Well, he wasn't biting.

The phone dinged again. His chest squeezed and he slowed to a walk as he yanked the phone from his pocket. He knew as well as anybody that she wouldn't stop texting until she got a response.

Greg: Where are you? Wedding breakfast is about to start.

He glanced at the boardwalk. He'd made it four and a half miles from the hotel. He checked the clock on his phone. One of his best running times this year. Who would have thought?

James: Boardwalk by Calliope's.

The restaurant made the best crab cakes in Belmont. In fact he'd hoped to take Kate there later this week.

His jaw twitched and he forced the thought away. Who knew what she was thinking? It wasn't his job to guess. Or to fix things for her. She knew her own mind; it was one of the things he loved most about her. If she'd run away, then it meant she wanted to be alone. Or at least away from him.

Love. The word hit him like a sucker punch to the gut.

Greg: Great, I'll drive down and pick you up. Mom wants to know where Kate is. Says she needs to talk to her about a gluten-free dinner menu for Thursday's family dinner.

His fingers clenched around the phone, so hard his knuckles turned white. He fought the urge to throw the stupid thing against the sand.

James: Kate went home. You break the news to Mom. I don't want to discuss it.

Three bubbles appeared on the screen, signaling Greg was drafting a message. He stared at them, his gut churning.

Greg: Will do. See you in five minutes.

He did a few stretches, then paced along the boardwalk, his eyes darting to the street every time a car whizzed by. What now? He'd go back to the hotel. Shower. Go home. And what?

Suddenly the idea of the day without Kate loomed large in front of him.

Fuck.

His brother's white Land Rover pulled up and the horn sounded. James shot him a glare and climbed into the passenger seat.

Greg looked him up and down. "You look like shit and you smell even worse. Tell me what happened."

He pulled his seat belt over his chest. "Just drive. I don't want to talk about it."

Greg paused, then shrugged. "Your loss. I was going to help you out with Mom, keep her busy. But I have the hangover

from hell so it'll probably just be easier for me to throw you
to Mom Wolf. If you don't want to talk about whatever happened to put you in such a damn shitty mood, that is."

The muscles in the back of his neck tensed. If forced to decide between his mother's prodding and Greg's, he'd prefer to
confide in his brother.

"She dated Nico Davidson."

Greg let out a long, low whistle. "No way. That guy's a dick."

He clenched his fists. He knew that.

Greg frowned. "I can't really picture them together, to tell
you the truth. He's so uptight. Straitlaced. And she's so not."

His temple throbbed. "I don't need an evaluation of their
relationship, thank you very much."

Greg huffed out a breath. "Fine, then. You want to tell me
what else happened? You didn't break up with her just because
she dated Nico, did you?"

He dropped his gaze to his hands. "Nope. I saw his name in
her phone, I asked her about it. She explained he was an ex. I
have to admit, I freaked out for a minute. The timing is weird,
with everything happening with Dad's business and her showing up in town. But she told me they broke up and I trust her."

Greg tapped his thumbs against the steering wheel. One of
his more obnoxious habits. "Did you tell her you trusted her?"

"Of course I did!" The words burst from him. Did his
brother think he was a total moron?

"OK. OK. Don't get your panties in a twist."

He scowled.

"So what happened after that?"

He rewound in his head. Then she'd looked at him, her arm

outstretched, her phone in her hand. Something had flickered over her eyes and then she'd shut down, as if a curtain had dropped. All of a sudden her expression had just closed.

"She ran. Like literally ran, down the beach and away from me."

Greg's eyebrows knit together. "She ran away from you? Huh. That is not what I would have expected."

He bit back an acerbic response. *Great. Thanks. Good talk.*

Instead he forced a shrug. "I guess I'm better off, right? Like if she's some crazy, wounded, damaged person then better to know now before things go too far. I'm not dating another Brooke."

Bile rose in his throat and he pushed it back down. Was Kate really like that? How could he have misread her so badly?

"Nah." Greg shook his head. "That doesn't seem like her."

As if either of them was an expert on understanding women. Maybe he'd been so caught up in who he wanted her to be that he'd ignored the red flags. Yet when he racked his brain, he couldn't come up with any.

"Running away didn't seem like her, either. Maybe, in the end, I would have felt as suffocated with her as I did with Brooke."

Greg turned into the hotel parking garage. He put the car in park before he turned to look at James. "Are you nuts? I've seen you with a lot of women this year and I have never, in my life or yours, seen you look at anyone the way you look at her."

His mouth went dry. His brother didn't know everything. He thought they were really dating.

"And I know you were just faking the relationship for Mom."

His head snapped up. "You did?"

Greg nodded. "Yup. The two of you were weird at that family dinner. But then she hurt herself and you rushed to her side and I saw it. You love her, man."

All the muscles in his back knotted. He did not love her. Besides, even if he did, it didn't matter.

"Don't be stupid."

Greg opened the driver-side door. "I'm not the stupid one. She doesn't have a dad, she doesn't have a mom, she lost her dream job less than six months ago. She's scared. Of course she's going to freak out a little. You need to give her time, let her have some room to figure it out."

The crushing sensation in his chest lightened and he looked to his brother. "Really? You really think so?"

Greg clapped a hand on his shoulder. "You don't trust my advice on women?"

He chuckled. He definitely didn't trust his brother's advice on women. But with any luck, Greg might be right.

CHAPTER TWENTY-THREE

Kate sat in the middle of the floor, Wally curled half on her lap with his fuzzy butt hanging off the back. All around her were shoeboxes and photo albums, pictures and videotapes. She lifted another VHS cassette and read the label. "Kate's third birthday." The swirling loops indicated her mother's handwriting.

Her heart squeezed and she set it aside. She'd have it converted to DVD and she'd give Rachel a copy. Maybe they could watch it together the next time she went to Philly.

Her eyes strayed to a blue-and-yellow-striped photo album and she flipped it open. The first photograph sucked the breath from her lungs. She wore dorky jean overalls while her sister was dressed in black leggings and a bedazzled frog T-shirt. Trendsetters, both of them. In between was their dad. His dark mustache curled on either side of his mouth as he wrapped them both in a hug. All three of them beamed at the camera.

The tears spilled over again and she gave in to them, letting her ribs ache as she sobbed. Why had she waited so long? Why had she tried to hide the sadness? Why had she thought she could power through her grief?

It was there, whether she acknowledged it or not. And it existed because everything before had been so wonderful. Thanksgiving dinners when the three of them played chef and concocted gourmet meals from recipes they'd found in the magazines. Summers when her dad took them to the beach and sat on the blanket, strumming his guitar while they ran into the waves and squealed.

His illness wasn't everything. Losing him wasn't everything. Somehow she'd let those two things overshadow the years of good memories that had come before.

With one last sob she pushed herself up from the floor.

Finally she was ready.

* * *

James kept the smile plastered to his face as he muddled through the crowd of guests. This was it. In thirty minutes the postwedding brunch would be over and he'd be free to do whatever the hell he wanted.

His head pounded. What he wanted was Kate. Her warm smile, her naked body, the two naps he'd promised her.

He felt himself growing hard again and had to fight the urge to punch himself in the stomach. This was stupid and useless. Greg was right. She had her own things to deal with. Until she did that, they couldn't be together.

He'd tried that once, with Brooke, and it had been a disaster. He couldn't make Kate happy unless she wanted to be happy.

For the billionth time he checked his phone. One thirty p.m. No missed calls. No incoming text messages. He clicked the e-mail icon, just in case.

Two new messages appeared in his in-box. "Sale on tailored suits," proclaimed one. "Work out smarter," said the other. He deleted them both.

From the corner of his eye he caught a flash of familiar sleek, dark hair. His heart pounded faster in his chest. It couldn't be her. Just a few hours ago she'd run away from him. Why would she be back?

He turned his head in the opposite direction, determined not to look. He knew it wasn't her. Why invite disappointment?

A familiar hand came to rest on his elbow and her orange scent filled his nose. He closed his eyes and inhaled deeply.

Kate.

"Can I talk to you?"

He turned toward her and alarm swept him as he processed her red, puffy eyes.

She'd been crying. *Shit.*

Without thinking he lifted a hand to touch her cheek. "Are you OK?"

Her eyes filled and she nodded quickly before she bit her lip and looked away. "Yeah. Can I talk to you somewhere in private, though?"

He led her through the crowd, making a path through the

people. Once they were in the hallway he glanced around until he found a small meeting room and pulled her inside, shutting the door behind them.

A lump formed in his throat as he watched her face. She'd definitely been crying.

She gave him a shaky smile. "I know you probably think I'm crazy and I'm not saying you'd be entirely wrong."

He opened his mouth to interrupt her, but she put a hand in front of herself, palm to him. "Wait. Let me finish."

He closed his mouth again.

"I miss my dad." Her chin wobbled and he stepped toward her, crushing her into his chest. Of course she did.

She took a deep breath. "And I'm scared. I've been thinking all morning and part of it is your family. You guys love each other and your mom has been so nice to me."

He almost chuckled. He'd never expected to hear those words from anyone's lips.

"I started to feel like I belonged. With the thing about Nico, I kind of panicked. I didn't want them all to hate me."

Clarity dawned. Of course she hadn't. But then why had she run?

"I would never let them hate you," he whispered into her hair.

She rested her palms on his chest and tilted her chin to him. "That's not the real reason I'm scared, though."

She dropped her eyes and swallowed hard. For a long moment she didn't speak.

Without thinking he opened his mouth. "I love you."

She froze in his arms before she lifted her eyes to his. They shone with moisture. "I love you." Then she narrowed her eyes. "I was going to say it first. You knew that, didn't you? You wanted to beat me to it…"

He crashed his mouth into hers and wound his arms around her waist. She melted into him, her tongue pushing into his mouth and tangling with his.

Just this once she'd have to let him win.

EPILOGUE

Six Months Later

She practically skipped from the courtroom, her heart racing. *RGB would walk calmly with her head held high. Like a classy lady.* She forced herself to put one foot in front of the other and keep the triumph from her face.

In the hall Mona wrapped her in a hug. "Congratulations. You should be very, very proud of yourself. Judge Glendale rarely convicts people of child abuse and even more rarely gives out that kind of jail time. Thanks to you, that little girl is safe."

Relief washed over her as her face stretched into a grin. It had been a long, hard week. She'd fought tooth and nail, and she'd won.

Mona gave her another squeeze before she released her. "Now go home and celebrate with that handsome boyfriend of yours. I hope he was something special planned."

Her pulse sped. She just wanted to see him. Funny how

after six months, the thought of spending the entire evening together still sent shivers down her spine. She hoped it would last forever.

On her way to the parking garage she pulled out her phone and texted James.

Kate: We won! Exhausted. Can't wait to see you.

James: You're a rock star. I'm so proud of you and can't wait to celebrate when you get home!

They'd moved into a new town house just outside the Point a month ago. Thanks to her new job with Mona, she knew she'd be staying in Belmont for a while.

Her heart leaped. Who knew? Maybe she'd be in Belmont for a long time.

She grinned to herself as she merged onto the highway and left the city behind.

When she reached the house she parked in one of their assigned spaces and rushed to the door. She unlocked it hurriedly and kicked her heels off in the foyer. Another benefit of owning a senior dog: Wally had never eaten a single pair of her shoes.

"Honey, I'm home!" she called.

James strode from the kitchen and swept her into a hug, twirling her in a circle. He planted a kiss on her lips and lowered her to the ground.

"How does it feel to be a successful, badass prosecutor?"

Her smile broadened until she felt as if her face might crack open. Adrenaline and happiness and exhaustion coursed through her body. She needed a glass of wine and a two-day nap, but she also felt as if she could dance all night.

So this was what it felt like to finally have everything she'd ever wanted.

Wally plodded up to her and leaned his giant head on her leg. She dropped a hand to give him a pat. Her life really was perfect.

The aroma of garlic wafted from the kitchen. "Something smells amazing."

She kissed him again and he wrapped his hands around her waist, pulling her close and deepening the kiss.

Heat pooled in her core. She couldn't get enough of him.

He gestured to the kitchen. "Dinner will be ready in a few minutes."

She kept her arms wrapped around him, unwilling to let him go. "Do you want to eat outside?"

It was unusually warm for March and she was determined to start making use of the back patio, which looked out on the ocean.

James planted a kiss on her forehead and turned back to the kitchen. "I already thought of that. Everything's ready. Go change."

She climbed the metal stairs to the master suite, with Wally padding behind her. When she'd thrown on some yoga pants and a tank top, she rejoined him in the kitchen.

"Are those scallops?" She leaned against his shoulder and peered into the pan. She loved being able to touch his strong, solid arms or lean against the hard muscles of his chest anytime she wanted.

"Your favorite. I made a special trip to Whole Paycheck." He flipped the sizzling scallops, showing one perfectly seared side. Her mouth watered.

"What's in the pot?" She moved to lift the lid, but he playfully swatted her hand away.

"Gluten-free ravioli."

Kate clapped in excitement. "Where did you get it?" She'd been stalking Whole Foods looking for gluten-free ravioli for months, but to no avail.

"I made it."

Her forehead furrowed. "I thought you had to work late."

He grinned. "I lied. I wanted to do something special for you."

Emotion tore through her. He'd bought scallops and made gluten-free ravioli, for her. Beth had been right, sometimes it was nice to let someone else take care of you. Every day, James showed her just how delicious letting go could be.

She wrapped her arms around him and rested her cheek against his back. "I love you."

He turned to face her, cupping her cheek. "I love you, too." He kissed her again. "But we'd better eat this before you distract me and it gets cold."

She nibbled his bottom lip, her pulse racing. "Threat or a promise?"

"Both." He held her gaze for a long moment before he turned back to the stove. "Now help me carry these outside."

She cracked open the French doors and took two plates

from him. When she stepped onto the patio, she gasped. Hundreds of Christmas lights twinkled and tea candles lined the porch railings. Two glasses and a bottle of champagne sat on the patio table.

Her eyes brimmed with tears. She didn't think she'd ever get used to all the small ways he found to show that he loved her.

"I told you I had it all taken care of." James grinned at her as he placed a bowl in the center of the table and pulled out her chair.

He grabbed the bottle of champagne and popped it open, pouring the frothy liquid into the two flutes. He put the bottle back in the ice bucket and held his glass out to her. "A toast to the sexiest prosecutor I know."

Her chest grew tight as she clinked her glass against his. He was perfect. This was perfect.

"You remember our first date?" His eyes held hers.

"Sushi?" They'd decided by mutual agreement to count it as their first date.

"Yes. Remember what we talked about?"

Kate raised an eyebrow. "Which part?"

"The part where you said you wanted a job you loved, to see your sister more, fabulous friends, and a boyfriend who adored you?"

"Yeah. I left out Wally." She beamed at him. She knew that wasn't what he meant. "I also said I was jealous of how two people could just fit together, just get one another. I couldn't find the right way to express what I meant, though."

James nodded. "You said it was maybe because you didn't know who you were." He reached across the table and ran a finger along the scar on her arm. When he got to her hand, he held it.

Kate let the tears spill over. Crying didn't scare her anymore. She knew now that whatever she felt, however she felt, she wouldn't be alone.

"What about now?" he asked.

"I think I always knew who I was, I was just scared to take the leap and be her." She took a deep breath. "Having you, knowing that you'll love me and support me no matter what, gives me the courage to be myself."

He smiled, his gray eyes alight. "I was thinking about that last night. I've been thinking about it a lot lately. We both said we wanted to find someone we fit with, who understood us. But I think the thing I couldn't put my finger on was how I wanted someone who understood me, who made me...more myself."

James leaned forward and held Kate's hands. "It's like the toast I gave at Morgan's wedding, the Mr. Rogers song. I love you. You're smart and sexy and opinionated and outspoken and beautiful and caring. Every day I discover something new about you that makes me love you even more than the day before. But more than that, I like you. I really, really, really like you. And I like who I am when I'm with you."

When he pushed out his chair and knelt in front of her, she could have sworn her heart stopped. His words floated to her and she had to concentrate to decipher them. She reached out to touch his face, just to make sure he was real. This was real.

"I need you to marry me."

Kate laughed.

"Katie, I'm not kidding. I'm not asking you or begging you or any of that. I'm telling you, I *need* you to marry me."

The dark intensity of his eyes pierced her. "I will marry you." She took his face in her hands and kissed him.

"Do you want to see the ring?" He plunged a hand into his pants pocket.

She laughed again. "I don't care if it's a Cracker Jack ring!"

"Laurie said you'd say that, but Mom wanted you to have it."

He snapped the box open and her breath caught. The center stone was a large blue sapphire. It was flanked by three small diamonds on each side, set in a white gold filigree band studded with smaller rectangular diamonds. She reached out a finger and tentatively touched it.

"Do you want to try it on?"

"It's for me?" Her voice quavered.

It was the most beautiful ring she'd ever seen.

"It was my grandma's. My mom saved it for you."

A lump formed in her throat and she stared at him, not trusting herself to respond. Margaret had saved it for her? Margaret wanted her to have it?

"Are you sure?"

"God, yes." He pulled her to him and kissed her, then slid it onto her finger. It fit perfectly.

Kate held out her hand and examined the ring. She turned it this way and that, unable to stop admiring it.

Her vision blurred and a fresh round of tears flowed down her cheeks.

James gathered her to him, holding her in his arms. "About that threat promise."

Kate laughed. James Abell was everything she needed and everything she'd ever wanted.

ACKNOWLEDGMENTS

Thank you to the many friends who supported and encouraged me during this process. Special thanks to Amanda Lanne-Camilli, my first beta reader, and to my critique partners Ekaterine Xia and Jules Dixon. You're crazy in all the best ways and I couldn't have done this without you. To my kind and wonderful agent, Dawn, who gives excellent advice. To Kelly Moran, who taught me so much about storytelling and deep point of view. To my editor, Michele, who makes me laugh and pushes me to be a better writer.

To my mom, for keeping all the books I made when I was seven, and to my dad, for being a tyrant on the subject of proper grammar. You're the best parents a girl could ask for.

And of course to my husband, Dan, for always being my wedding date. Even when I embarrass him and dance the chicken dance.

Single dad Griffin Hall has traded late-night gigs and partying for bedtime stories with his little girl in his arms. So when Beth Beverly comes into his coffee shop with her big heart and delicious sweet treats, she makes him feel alive again. But there's a little secret Beth doesn't know about his past. Will this former bad boy lose the one woman he can't let go of?

Look for the next book by Kelly Eadon, available in July 2016. A preview follows.

CHAPTER ONE

Beth Beverly adjusted the wings strapped to her back, balanced the box on her hip, and slammed the heel of her hand into the door to the coffeehouse.

Thud thud thud.

Sarah would flip her lid. It had been years since they'd founded Belmont College for the Arts' annual Halloween contest, but you were never too old to dress up. Real dress-up, not slutty bunny, slutty genie, slutty waitress or maid or whatever dress-up. Those had their time and place, but this wasn't it.

She bounced on the balls of her feet as she imagined her college friend's reaction. It would be epic. With any luck Sarah would be in costume, too.

Her antennae swayed back and forth and she prayed they'd hold up through the day. She had a lot of muffin deliveries to make.

The door jerked open. Griffin Hall towered over her, his

eyebrows furrowing on his otherwise perfect face. Her heart lodged in her stomach as his eyes pierced her. She swallowed hard, her eyes taking in the dark-blond hair that curled over the corners of his ears and the few days' worth of facial hair on his chin.

Where was Sarah? Her hot sourpuss boss wasn't Beth's intended audience. Suddenly she wished she'd gone with slutty…something. Anything sexier than a bumblebee. Then again, weren't most things sexier than a bumblebee?

"Ummm." Her throat was scratchy. "Muffin delivery?"

He stepped to the side and held the door open with one sinewy arm.

OK, then.

"You guys having a good morning?" She eased past him and into the back prep area of the bustling coffeehouse. The smell of dark roast coffee enveloped her, causing her mouth to water. A clamor of voices drifted from the front service area. His business was always hopping and he was always stone-faced. She'd never been able to make sense of his brooding demeanor.

After all, her business had bombed catastrophically two years ago and she still found plenty of reasons to smile.

You don't know his backstory.

Maybe his family had been lost at sea and he was the sole survivor. Or maybe he was a coffee shop owner who hated mornings. Or maybe he belonged to some weird cult that required he wear mohair underwear. Whatever it was, Griffin carried something heavy.

"Sure. Been pretty busy." His voice was a low rumble. In spite of his dark expression, her stomach flipped.

Stop that.

Griffin had never said more than a handful of words to her, even though she'd delivered baked goods to his doorstep every Monday and Wednesday morning for months. So what if his lean frame, dirty-blond hair, and sage eyes made her weak in the knees? Someday, when she had more than a few seconds to spare, she'd find a way to make him smile.

Today, while she stood before him as a bumblebee, was not that day. Besides, she had a dozen deliveries to make before 8:00 a.m.

She lifted the lid of the box so he could see inside. "One dozen carrot cake, one dozen lemon corn, and one dozen good old chocolate chip. Think that'll get you through?"

He'd never failed to sell out of her muffins. Ever. But she was picky about the shops she worked with and she artfully dodged requests that she expand her production. One failed business per lifetime was sufficient and she was perfectly content working as a part-time baker, part-time kids' drama teacher, part-time seamstress, part-time whatever.

"Yeah, that should work." His irises took on a blue hue and for the hundredth time she wondered what that meant. She scanned his forehead, cheeks, chin, jaw, eyebrows. Usually she was good at reading people, intuiting their emotional states. But with Griffin? Nothing. Nada. Zip.

Beth peeked into the dining room, where people crowded around tables and waited in line. Little Ray of Sunshine was a haven for people from every walk of life: local wannabe artists, bikers, stay-at-home moms, starving actors, and high school athletes. It was one of the things that intrigued her most about him.

She turned back, only to find his eyes fixed on her intently. A fire ignited low in her stomach and she had to focus to keep her breathing steady. Rather than looking away, he met her gaze.

You're dressed like a flipping bumblebee!

Sarah entered from the storage area. "Beth!"

Now she shows up.

Sarah blinked at her, then dissolved into laughter, grasping her sides as she heaved for breath. "Again? The bee?"

Beth stuck her tongue out. So she hadn't won the BCA contest that year in college. It was still an awesome costume and she couldn't let it go to waste.

Sarah folded her into a hug. "You're the only person I know who can still fit into clothes from freshman year."

"Eh." Beth shrugged. "I don't know that anyone would call this clothes." She waved at her torso, which was ensconced in yellow and black stripes. Who cared what the fashion police said? Horizontal stripes would come back in eventually.

Sarah rolled her eyes. "Did you bring us any goodies?"

They were in her van, parked out back. She always made sure to bring goodies for the staff.

She winked at her friend. "Of course. Griffin, care to join us?"

Today's baked goods had been designed with him in mind and she couldn't trust Sarah to escort them all safely back inside.

The left side of his mouth quirked up and her pulse raced. A smile! Or almost a smile. She'd been trying to worm one out of him for weeks.

"I'd love to." He opened the door and held it while they both walked through. As Beth passed him she caught a whiff of coffee and caramel and something manly and musky. Her heart thumped.

Sarah dragged her by the hand in the direction of the van, her purple hair streaming behind her.

"Ooooh." She paused to look through the window of the van, admiring a dress that hung from a hook in the back. "Where did you get that?"

"The fabric? Finders Keepers." It was a thrift store they'd long been obsessed with. When she saw the green cotton printed with tiny squirrels she'd had to snap it up.

"Hey, Griffin, don't you think May would die for a dress like that?"

May? Beth's spine stiffened. So he did have a girlfriend. Or maybe even a wife. Plenty of restaurant people didn't wear rings at work.

Griffin leaned to peer through the window. "She'd love it."

He turned to face her and his eyes sparkled, but still no full-blown smile. "You make it in four-year-old size?"

A daughter. The knot in her stomach loosened only slightly. Daughters had mothers, after all.

She reached for the handle to the van's door, which creaked as she tried to pry it open. Poor Martha had seen a lot of use over the years and wasn't getting any younger.

"Need some help?" His arm brushed against hers, making her skin sing with awareness.

She abruptly stepped away from the door. "Um, sure. Just be

careful with Martha. She's getting up there and she requires a delicate touch sometimes."

He raised an eyebrow. "Martha, eh?"

"Like Martha Stewart. The hostess with the mostest. Hostess CupCakes. Baking. Maybe you have to be drunk, but it seemed fitting at the time." She and her friends Kate and Ryan had gotten drunk once during a snowstorm and tossed around stupid names for their future businesses. Ryan's record label was named Hungry Hippo, her van was Martha, and none of them could look at a bottle of Jack Daniel's ever again.

His mouth lifted into a real, genuine smile and her skin broke into goose bumps. With a pointed look her way, he eased the door open. She ducked her head inside the van to grab a small box, which she shoved into Griffin's hands. Now that he'd shown a glimmer of an emotion other than annoyance, her stomach was like a fireworks display.

He held a finger out to her, a smattering of silver and purple sparkles flecking the surface. She racked her brain. Glitter? What had she made recently?

There were certain things she'd never outgrow, and glitter was definitely one of them. Glitter *and* costumes.

She shrugged. "I don't ask where Martha goes or what she does at night. I try not to pry into her private life."

He laughed, a low rumble.

Mentally she patted herself on the back. A real smile and a laugh. And they hadn't even gotten to the contents of the box yet.

"What did you bring us?" Sarah snatched it from Griffin's hand.

"Lemon squares. I found some Meyer lemons at the store the other day." By "found" she meant she'd hunted through four local supermarkets until she'd located the perfect ones. It was imperative that these particular lemon squares be the best she'd ever made.

"My favorite." Griffin shifted his weight and stared at his feet, his eyes hooded.

She shrugged. She already knew they were his favorite. One of his staff had let it slip and the tidbit had haunted her into lemon-hunting submission. Once she got an idea in her head, she had to create the vision or it would drive her mad.

At least that was the excuse she was going with. The fact that Griffin was dead sexy in a rugged-logger kind of way had made her challenge all the more imperative.

"You find a new roommate yet?" Sarah shoved a lemon square into her mouth, sending crumbs flying from her lips.

"Nah. I'm just sort of seeing." It was a stupid approach, given her financial history. But she'd crunched the numbers a million different ways and she could afford to live by herself. Besides, she had a feeling that the universe would bring her the perfect roommate.

Her heart twinged at the idea of letting someone else move into Kate's room. She was happy her best friend was madly in love, but she missed seeing her every day. There was a certain kind of intimacy you experienced only when you saw someone at her drunkest, sleepiest, craziest, and crankiest. She wasn't sure she was ready to take that leap with someone new.

Kate was right, maybe she should get a dog.

"My cousin's looking for a place. I'll talk to her and get in touch with you. What's the rent?"

Beth threw out the number along with some pertinent info: the location by the beach, the small backyard, the awesome porch. Plus free samples of all baking experiments. The only requirement was that her new roomie tolerate clutter. The entire house had morphed into her workshop.

Beth glanced at her watch and her heart lurched. Almost 7:00 a.m. She and Martha had better get back to their regularly scheduled deliveries.

"I'll see you guys next week. Get ready for some exciting new muffin flavors! I've been experimenting." That was another reason she loved Little Ray of Sunshine. It sold whatever muffins she brought it, no questions asked. It had even managed to sell out of her chipotle chocolate.

"Thanks for the lemon squares." Griffin had closed the box and held it firmly under one arm, out of Sarah's reach.

"Anytime." She winked and climbed into the van, not pausing to see his expression. She prayed it was another hard-earned smile.

* * *

She'd caught him staring. He was always so careful not to be caught, not to give her any hint of the way her body infiltrated his thoughts all day, and she'd caught him staring.

Maybe she'll chalk it up to the bumblebee costume.

After all, it was pretty crazy. And, from what he'd heard, exactly the kind of thing Beth would do. Most of his staff had gone to Belmont College for the Arts and it was a small town.

He recalled her short, curly hair and the way her eyes had danced as her pink lips formed the words *lemon squares.* Adrenaline shot through his veins. He'd pictured that look so many times.

What would his bandmates think if they could see him now? Single father, living in a beach town and pining after the local baker…who just happened to be dressed as a bee.

He chuckled to himself. They'd never believe it. Hell, sometimes even he couldn't believe it. Only a few years ago he'd been playing sold-out shows in Japan and now he woke up at 4:00 a.m. to brew coffee for the masses.

"May really would look cute in a dress like that. Maybe Beth would make one for you? She's good with stuff like that."

The mention of his four-year-old daughter brought Griffin crashing back to reality. The judge had unequivocally granted him custody and he was determined to prove her right. He was, and always would be, the best guardian for Mabel. So what if it meant permanently shelving his dream of a career as a musician?

He clenched his fists. *Mabel is happy. Mabel will be happy.* His daughter would grow up normal, emotionally healthy, happy, and unscarred. These days he'd probably settle for minimally scarred. Raising a kid could be damn hard.

"You're not moving your cousin in with Beth." He spun on his heel and headed for the door. His footsteps pounded on the pavement.

"Why not?" Sarah had given up her help-my-jailbird-cousin routine with him weeks ago.

"Because your cousin is a convicted felon."

He held the door open and Sarah stepped through. "Beth doesn't care about those kinds of things. She's, you know, cool?"

He gritted his teeth. His staff relied on him to be uncool, the same way his daughter did. That was how he kept them employed, which meant they were fed and clothed.

"I'm not going to have this conversation with you again, Sarah." Of course he was. Eventually he had to get it through her thick skull that the world wasn't some magical la-la land where everything worked out. It wasn't pessimism, it was realism, and he'd had to learn the hard way.

His temple throbbed. What was it with the creative types? Had he been like this, too? Before Mabel?

"She's my cousin, Griff." Her use of his nickname signaled that she knew he was right. She'd asked him to hire her cousin only once before she'd given up. His decisions weren't up for debate.

"And she sold stolen property and served two years in jail. I can't trust her to work here, and you shouldn't trust her to live with your friend. Beth's your friend, don't take advantage of her." His chest constricted. Bad things happened to people like Beth.

He followed Sarah into the coffee shop, where she ripped open the box and began to arrange the muffins on a tray to be placed in the display case. They'd be sold out within two hours, as usual. "Mandi's boyfriend conned her into selling stolen property and she took the fall for him because she's stupid and love is blind."

He groaned. "Actions speak louder than words."

If you wanted to judge a person's character, you looked to the things they'd done in their lives. If you didn't know the things they'd done in their lives, then you didn't trust until they'd proved trustworthy. Why was he the only one in possession of any common sense? Frustration flared inside him.

Going through the courts was a tedious nightmare, but they got things right. If Mandi had been convicted, then she was guilty.

Sarah tugged at a strand of hair. She should have been wearing it up around the food, but he'd long ago given up telling her what to do.

"She had a shitty childhood."

A vein in his temple throbbed. Lots of people had shitty childhoods and managed to be productive members of society. You couldn't use the shit life threw at you as an excuse for bad decisions.

Look at him. His life was nothing like what he'd expected and he had nobody to blame but himself. He worked constantly, never had enough time with his daughter, and worried every damn day that he'd screw her up. The only thing that eased the web of anxiety in his chest was her smile.

And his daydreams of Beth.

He shook his head. No more thoughts of Beth. If she kept making lemon squares and walking ahead of him, her hips swaying hypnotically, his willpower would break. And he couldn't afford any more complications in his life.

CHAPTER TWO

Mabel sat at a stool at the counter, singing for a leather-clad fiftysomething biker.

"Then the princess climbed up the ladder...," she trilled, inventing the words as she went along.

Like father, like daughter. Maybe she was destined to be a musician, too.

Wisps of blond hair escaped from her French braids and he reminded himself to buy sturdier hair ties. The ones with the rubber grips on the insides. A mom at Mabel's preschool had said that they worked the best for "active" children.

Mabel was most certainly active.

He handed a cappuccino to the next woman in line. She'd asked for low-fat milk and he'd had to explain, politely, that he didn't serve that kind of swill to his customers. Sure it was the latest fad, but people would be over it soon enough. He couldn't be remembered as serving crap coffee, otherwise how would his business survive the highs and lows? No, it was better to stick to his principles.

She took a sip. "This is the best cappuccino I've ever had."

Damn straight it was. People forgot that things tasted like cardboard when you removed any trace of fat. He carried only whole milk and people could take it or leave it. "In the mornings we have really good muffins, too."

"Muffin?" Mabel's ears perked up. The kid loved muffins. Especially Beth's mango-chili ones.

"Not tonight, May." It was nearly dinnertime and he should get her back to the house and fix her something that could pass for a healthy meal. The child psychologist he'd consulted said Mabel needed to spend time around other adults, although he was pretty sure the coffee shop crowd wasn't what she had in mind.

"I love muffins," she whispered to the preppy high school student seated on the other side of her.

"Me, too," the girl whispered back.

This. This was why he loved Little Ray of Sunshine. Where else would so many different people have a chance to come together? Where else could his daughter learn firsthand the diversity that existed in the world? Warmth flooded him. He needed to remember this feeling when he was awake at 2:00 a.m. reviewing purchasing orders. Or when a customer stormed out because he refused to make a triple-shot hazelnut macchiato, room temperature, with half soy and half skim milk, chocolate flakes on top, and caramel drizzle.

The bell on the door jingled and he glanced to see Ryan walk through. A redhead followed him in and surveyed the shop.

"Hey, man." Ryan strode to the counter and clapped a hand in Griffin's. Ryan managed a local band, Vibe Riot. Griffin had met Ryan when he'd booked the band to do one of the coffeehouse's local art and music Friday nights. He knew how hard it could be to get your big break and he wanted to pay it forward.

Griffin pulled a cup to prepare Ryan's usual order. Caffè Americano, with an extra shot of espresso. The guy was almost as much of a caffeine addict as he.

"Who's your friend?"

The woman stood a few feet away by the door, her eyes glued to Ryan. Sarah said he had that Abercrombie model look going on that girls loved. Griffin wondered how many gallons of hair gel he went through in a week. Having so much of the stuff in close proximity to your brain couldn't be healthy, could it?

"Allie." Ryan motioned in her direction. "She'll have a nonfat cappuccino."

"Don't have the nonfat shit."

Ryan gave him a nod. "I know, but nobody has to tell her that, right?"

He chuckled. While he didn't necessarily believe in lying, a little omission could be for the greater good. Preserving coffee integrity was definitely a worthy cause and nonfat was an abomination to cappuccinos everywhere.

"What are you up to tonight?" The pitcher of milk spluttered as he submerged it under the steamer.

Ryan always stopped by for an afternoon coffee before setting off to a show or a night of drinking.

"Checking out a new band in Stonyfield. Friend of Allie's."

He winked at Griffin. "You want to come with?"

Sarah sidled up beside him. "Oh, you should. A bunch of us are going. We can carpool if you want?"

He sighed and rolled his shoulders, trying to ease the knots in his back. "Can't. Couldn't find a sitter."

Another harmless lie. Much as he missed the nightlife and having friends outside of work, that wasn't for him anymore. Loud concerts at the Black Cat and shooting whiskey until the sun rose couldn't hold a candle to his baby girl falling asleep in his arms. Or her pleas for just one more story.

Besides, he cringed to remember how his pre-Mabel lifestyle had been portrayed by Angela's parents in court. Nope, that kind of thing wasn't for him anymore.

"My cousin could probably do it," Sarah volunteered.

His stomach clenched. No way. He'd never leave Mabel with someone he didn't know, much less a convicted felon.

Sarah must have read the look on his face because she sighed impatiently. "Not Mandi. The one who runs a day care."

His jaw remained tense. Tonight was his time with Mabel, to tell her stories and tuck her into bed. It was the single best part of his day. "That's nice of you to offer, but I promised her daddy-and-daughter time."

Sarah placed a hand on his arm. "You're the best dad, you know that?"

He turned his face so she couldn't read his expression. "Not the best, but I'm trying."

Sarah squeezed his arm tighter. "The very fucking best. I know it."

Ryan reached forward to claim his coffees. "This is a

really sweet moment, and I'm sure you're a kick-ass dad, but I need to get on the road. Give me a buzz if you change your mind."

It was one of the reasons they'd become friends. Ryan never questioned his personal life or passed judgment. He was exactly the kind of friend Griffin needed these days.

"Oh, and I brought you this." Ryan reached into his pocket and brought out a thumb drive, which he pressed into Griffin's hand.

"Demo?" Griffin eyed it expectantly. Ryan had good taste in bands and had clued him in on a couple of up-and-comers. He'd worried he would miss that kind of networking when he'd left the industry, but he'd found a way to use the coffee shop to stay connected to the music business.

"A mix I thought you might like. Good for the car ride home. Let me know what you think."

Ryan raised a hand good-bye and sidled out the door, his newest lady friend in tow.

Griffin turned his attention to Mabel. "All right, Mabel, say good-bye to your friends, please." She knew more of the customers' names than he did and he had a suspicion that most of the afternoon crowd stopped by specifically to see her.

She pouted but jumped off the stool and shuffled to a nearby table. "Good-bye Mary, good-bye Sam, good-bye Thunder…" Griffin glanced at the grizzled old man who was hunched over a cup he was fairly certain contained a good dose of whiskey. Was that really the guy's name?

The man grunted back at Mabel with a smile. Huh. Maybe his name was Thunder.

"Daddy!" Mabel's voice reverberated through the noisy coffee shop.

He gave her a pointed look. "I'm coming. What did I say about inside voices?"

"Inside voices are overrated!" She hadn't adjusted her volume and the customers in the shop burst into laughter, which made her beam triumphantly in his direction. Where had she learned the word *overrated*? Did she know what it meant?

He couldn't help himself. A low laugh escaped him. So much for not encouraging bad behavior. His girl had a future as an actress or a comedian. Definitely something that involved the stage.

His brain pinged with a faint memory. Crap. Kid theater classes started in a few days and he'd totally forgotten to sign her up. Some dad he was. He'd have to check the website when she went to bed and pray they still had a spot open.

He sighed, crossed the room to Mabel, and scooped her up. Her arms wrapped around his neck and her head lay heavy on his shoulder, the scent of her baby shampoo lingering in the air.

Once he'd strapped her into her car seat, he plugged the thumb drive into his adapter. A file named "For the Kid" appeared on his phone screen. Maybe Ryan was a softy after all. He clicked.

Kasey Musgraves filled the car with a song about biscuits. In the backseat Mabel nodded and hummed along. When it ended there were a few seconds of dead air before heavy metal began to blast.

"I eat you in your face! I smash you in your face! I am a cannibal! I am a cannibal!" He slammed on the brakes and jerked the car to the shoulder, then punched the pause button on his phone and glanced in the rearview mirror.

His chest pounded and his heart raced. How was that a kid-appropriate song?

In the backseat Mabel was giggling. "You can't eat someone's face! They're silly, Daddy. There's no such thing as a can animal."

He breathed a sigh of relief. Freaking Ryan and his practical jokes.

* * *

Beth clutched the ice cream cone in one hand and dug through her purse with the other. She located a wad of bills and tried to shove one in the tip jar, but they scattered across the counter.

"Beth. He's not a stripper. You can't go around throwing money at people." Kate pressed her lips into a line, a sure sign she was trying not to smile.

"Says who?" she shot back.

Her best friend burst into laughter.

"Everyone likes tips," she added as she shoved the wallet back into her purse.

The employee's back was to them, but by the way the tips of his ears turned red she had a feeling he'd heard the exchange.

"Thank you!" she called cheerily to him as they walked out the door.

They swapped ice cream cones for a second, so they could

sample one another's flavors. She'd even gotten a gluten-free cone, so her friend wouldn't feel left out.

Coffee caramel exploded on her tongue, but she was glad she hadn't chosen it for herself. The balance of sweet to bitter had never struck her as right. Bubble gum was the way to go. Pure sweetness.

"I think you traumatized that poor kid."

Kate grinned and handed Beth's cone back. "Twenty dollars says I made his day by implying people would pay to see him naked."

Beth chuckled. Traumatized and flattered weren't mutually exclusive.

They picked their way down a path to the beach and she inhaled the salty sea air. Belmont was so much better in the fall when residents didn't have to dodge a crush of out-of-town beachgoers.

"What was yesterday's baking project?" Kate kicked off her shoes and wiggled her toes in the sand.

"Lemon squares."

"Yeah? And who were your latest victims?" Kate knew she liked to spread cheer in the form of baked goods.

"Griffin, the guy who owns Little Ray of Sunshine downtown."

"Griffin, eh? And why does he own a bakery named after you?"

Normally she would have come up with a snappy reply to the quip about her size, but her mind was miles away. He'd retained possession of her thoughts for a full thirty six hours. She'd tried to compile the little he'd shared about himself over the last few months, but her mental list was barely sufficient to fill a Post-it: Owns a coffee shop. Has a four-year-old daughter named May. No wedding ring. No mention of a girlfriend. Doesn't smile. Always at work at the crack of dawn. Likes lemon squares and…?

Kate stopped walking and cocked her head to the side as she examined Beth. "Spill."

That's what twenty-plus years of friendship got her. Kate could see directly into her head and vice versa.

"Drop-dead gorgeous. All muscle, kind of blondish hair, strong shoulders. Exactly the right amount of stubble." Her skin heated and she reached to fluff her short, curly hair so it partially covered her face.

"That sounds promising."

Her stomach twisted. "I hope so. He doesn't talk a lot."

Kate's dark eyes danced. "Oooh, the strong, silent type? So what's his deal?"

She shrugged. "No clue. I think he maybe has a kid?"

"That's also promising. Kids love you. Maybe that's your in?"

She bit her lip. Yeah, she'd been thinking about him nonstop, reviewing his slight deviations in facial expression in an attempt to determine the emotions they represented. Still, she wasn't sure where any of this was going and the fact that he owned his business tied her stomach in knots. She was bad news for small businesses, a dark cloud of doom. She had the bankruptcy papers and shitty credit history to prove it. Maybe she should leave Griffin and his successful business alone.

"Maybe."

Kate faced her and stared into her eyes. "Yeah, you're right. I have a better idea. You should dress up as a human lemon square and invite him to lick you all over. Go straight to X-rated, no kid-friendly stuff allowed."

The laughter came bubbling out and her shoulders relaxed.

A human lemon square sounded delicious. She'd have to store the idea away in case things with Griffin did progress. "I do think he was staring at me today…"

"Of course he was!" Kate grabbed her hand and squeezed. "So, he's dark and brooding? Like Mr. Rochester?"

Beth wrinkled her nose. She'd never loved *Jane Eyre*. It was dismal and depressing, full of pain and suffering. She was more of a fairy-tale kind of girl herself. The Disney versions, not the Brothers Grimm.

Kate examined her face. "Right. No *Jane Eyre* for you…What about 'Beauty and the Beast'? He's the growling, cursed prince, and you're the one who can show him the light?"

She let out a low chuckle. "He's too good-looking to be the Beast."

Kate winked. "Well, you never know what's going on underneath that brooding expression. I think you should find out."

This sent her into another fit of giggles. "Oh, believe me, I want to."

"Let's make a plan!" Kate crunched the last bite of her cone. They'd reached their favorite pier, where they'd watch the orange sun set over the water.

Beth sighed. "Remember how you met James when you deviated from the plan and let life happen?"

"Remember how you told me to get off my ass, stop being scared, and give life a chance to make things happen?"

Zing. One point for Kate.

She shrugged. It couldn't hurt to hear her out. "Why not? Lay it on me."

She listened as she bit into the gluten-free ice cream cone and sugar coated her tongue. She was only half listening to the details of Kate's plan as her mind wandered back to Griffin and his dark-green eyes. The universe would do its thing, she was sure of it, and everything would come out right. It always did.

CPSIA information can be obtained
at www.ICGtesting.com
Printed in the USA
BVOW04s2120230317
479339BV00001B/11/P